MW00908858

WEB NEAR SOUP

Philip Denisch

This book is a work of fiction.
Names, characters, places, and incidents are the product
of the author's imagination. Any resemblance to actual
events, locales, or persons living or dead is purely
coincidental.

Web Near Soup

Third Edition

Copyright © 2014 by Philip Denisch

All rights reserved.

CHAPTER ONE

HISTORY

A sweetened, condensed history of the town of Boudton. Skipping past the Silurian and Cambrian epochs and their varied creatures, the first human resident of Boudton was Jacob Bunsen. He wasn't born in Boudton as it didn't exist yet. Rather, he was the first one who came and stayed there. He was born and raised in a land far away. The town he was born in wasn't a very comfortable place. The work was hard, the people surly, and the rulers capricious.

He was chosen by his family to find a better place where they all could live. A new land had been discovered recently and it was decided that he should go and prepare a place where they could live more comfortably. So he left the place of his birth and everything he had ever known. Monies were collected from his parents, aunts, uncles, and cousins, and entrusted to Jacob. They all gave as much as the poor farmers and trappers could for a fresh start in a new place.

After a three day's walk with his strongest cousin as guide and bodyguard, he arrived in the closest town with a port. It was a little city on the edge of a giant ocean. It smelled of fish left out in the sun too long and of bodies left without soap too long, quite foreign from the smell of offal left in the dirt too long and the bodies never knowing soap that he was familiar with. He booked passage from a wiry man with very long eyebrows and said good-bye to his cousin. He only had to stay alone in the city one night, though he barely slept from clutching the bag of money tied around his waist.

In the morning, with the sun barely a smudge through the smoke of the city's thousand small fires, he boarded the ship that would take him across the angry sea to his new home. The creaking, sloshing barque took him further away from his place of birth than any of his ancestors. He relished the thought of starting anew, though was sobered by the realization that a large portion of everyone he ever knew were counting on him. It was his job to prepare a place for them in the wild, untamed expanse of a strange, new land.

The motion of the vessel bothered him for only a few days. The young, but tanned and weather-beaten façade won back over the recent greenish hue brought about by the boat's motion. He enjoyed the bright skies and fascinating water. It was like the most barren desert he could ever have imagined. Instead of an endless stretch of sand and rock, it was an endless stretch of undrinkable water. Only rarely did he see something break the surface. There were small, half-fish, half-bird-like things that jumped and glided across the tops of waves and the huge, frighteningly large whales that swiped only the tops of their backs above the dark green water.

In the city where he disembarked, he worked on clearing out his accent in the new language. Those who knew it back home had taught him, but spoke it in a rather peculiar way. He set about his task of preparing a place for his family and learned all he could about this fresh country. After months of talking to travelers and studying every map he could find, he secured a meeting with a large land-owner and made an offer on a parcel of land. It cost him most of the family's accumulated savings.

On a cool, brilliantly lit, spring day he set off. He gathered his meager personal belongings, said goodbye to the people he had met in the bustling city and headed west.

He passed through a number of towns along the way, and bought supplies and tools that he would need once he had arrived at his chosen location. In a village called Conville he spent a

little more time than at the others, as he had met
a woman named Edwina. They quickly realized a
mutual admiration for each other. She admired
him for bravely undertaking the adventure
before him. He admired her confidence and
charm. They agreed that if he could secure his
home and last the winter, she would entertain a
proposal of marriage the next spring. He
marched out the West Road for a few more days'
journeying until he found the surveyors mark.
Another half day's travel and he turned north off
the road, more of a path really at this point, and
into the dark of the forest. A few hours into the
thickly wooded land he found a level area
suitable to build a homestead.

He cleared enough land for a house and some
more to plant the crops he knew would be
needed for the long, cold winter. The soil was
not that much different from what he had
known in his homeland. The loam was dark and
rich. The stumps left by his axe were tough and
did not give up their foothold easily, but with
perseverance he cleared enough land for a first
crop. Between his small fields and the bountiful
hunting the woods provided he knew he'd be
able to survive the winter.

His next task was the building of a home and
barn. For the house, he built the first room of a

planned large house. It would have to be large enough to hold his entire family when they arrived in a few years, but one room was all he needed for now. The barn was next, storage for the fruits of his harvest and for the oxen he would get next spring to expand the farm. The barn was finished just in time for his first harvest and the harvest was finished just as the first leaves of autumn dropped from the trees. The forest around him exploded in a splash of colors. Every tree around him was dripping orange, red, yellow, brown and every hue in between. The winds came next and cleared the remaining clothing from the verdure. The tall, stout trees creaked in their emptiness as the gusts turned colder and colder. During the months of snow he burned the collected firewood, hunted, and planned the farming lands. He enjoyed the solitude but remained hopeful that Edwina would still consent to be his wife in the spring. This would be a fine place to raise a family.

Early the next spring he journeyed back to Conville. Edwina was overjoyed to see Jacob return, and she was still agreeable to his proposal of marriage. The fact that her family was poor and there would be no dowry did not bother him in the least. Her sunny disposition, capable manner and general knowledge of life were what he was interested in. The fact that they were also in love only made the situation sweeter.

They were married by the town preacher, enjoyed a small wedding-day party thrown by her relatives and friends and set off right away for their new home. A teary farewell from her mother and father made the journey to her new home a bittersweet trail.

They worked very hard the next year preparing for the arrival of his family. Each bright morning made her feel more at home. Each chore completed connected her more closely with this place. Each evening's meal spent talking of the day's accomplishments and tomorrow's plans brought them closer together. Every other month they would travel to Conville to catch up on news and visit. They celebrated the day he posted a letter to his home country telling his waiting family it was time for them to come over. A toast from their only bottle of wine punctuated the moment.

They grieved six months later when they heard the ship his whole family had sailed on was wrecked - all hands lost at sea. They were in Conville visiting her family and it was the nearest town with post service. With sad hearts

they went back to their home. They never visited
her home town again for she had come to think
of this man and his family as her own. Every
evening before sleeping they would lie in bed
and he would regale her with tales of his family
back in the old country. The loss was devastating
to them both. But it did not ruin them. Their
resolve was even stronger now. The whole job
was theirs. It was up to them alone to wrest a
living place for themselves and the family that
would come from them. Not soon after, they
started a new family of their own. The years
passed and they were happy.

Other families moved into the area. The Bunsens
would sell a piece of land for a farm or a store
and pretty soon a small town had grown just
past where their own farm was.

Jacob died while plowing a field for corn. Edwina
and their children gave him a simple burial in
the graveyard they started with his tomb. She
soon followed and was laid beside him. Others
from the town, now called Boudton, were buried
there as well. The quiet hillock out a ways from
the crossroads gently held them all in calm
repose year after year.

Time passed, horses gave way to automobiles,
wood gave way to gas, and then electricity, and

the older generation gave way to the newer. The town of Boudton grew and changed. An occasional fire would get one building replaced with another, or two would combine, or split. Babies were born, children moved out, new people moved in. The Bunsen family, fairly wealthy now from selling parcels of the original land stopped farming. Much of their land was now filled with houses, stores, or other buildings. John of the third generation even planted trees where his forefather had worked so hard to remove them. In town there were discussions on whether Jacob was doing some spinning in his grave or not. But the trees were pretty and no one resented his right to plant trees on his own land. Most of the family money had been spent by the time John got married. He married Sue Johnson, a daughter of another old family to the town. Sue worked in town, part-time, at Mrs. Tonsor's Hair Salon. It was more barbershop than salon, but plenty of people, both men and women enjoyed the service and atmosphere. Their only other income came from the small hardware store where one of Jacob's original shovels was hung on the wall. John and Sue had a daughter. When Sue died unexpectedly, John sold the store, wanting to spend more time raising their daughter, Mariel. The last of his money went with his daughter Mariel to college. Mariel never came back, and only called once to tell her father she was getting married, and to have him send the rest of her belongings to an address in the city.

The hardware store was sold to Mr. Palti, an escapee, he would say, from the city. He fell right into the flow of the town, never missing the hustle and bustle of the city. The slower, calmer attitude of the small town was much more agreeable to him. John Bunsen would still come by the store, almost daily, to give advice or just hang out. He wanted that connection with others, now that his daughter was gone. Mr. Palti didn't mind, he enjoyed the old man's company.

One day in early autumn when John hadn't been by the store in a few days, Mr. Palti got worried. He asked Chief Jardem of the town's police department to join him in going out to check on old Mr. Bunsen as he hadn't looked well the last few weeks. They found him slouched in his rocking chair on the screened-in porch on the back of the house. His empty eyes looked out over the trees he had planted years ago. His eyes were open, but his soul had closed up and moved on. The chief found Mariel's phone number in an address book in the kitchen. The page with her number on it looked as if it had never been turned to. Whether from never being called or knowing the number by heart Chief

Jardem didn't know.

When they laid him to rest on the grassy hillock, in good company with his ancestors, the clouds opened up and the rain came down. He, being the last of the name Bunsen. Everyone felt sure the town was weeping for its founding family. John's daughter Mariel didn't attend the funeral and Chief Jardem knew then the page with her number was unwrinkled from never having been used.

Mariel sent movers and an antiques expert who hauled away all the old furniture, some from the very founding of the town. The bureaus, chests, and chairs bought for Jacob's family that sat barren for years waiting for owners that never came were eventually used and worn by the later generations. Many other pieces from throughout the years were packed up and moved off. They were taken to an auction house in the city. Mariel sent lawyers to handle the estate. She sold the remaining land to a developer for new houses. A few people in town were upset, saying an era was over, but few truly begrudged Mariel the right to deal with her father's estate as she chose.

The developer's men and machines came the next spring. A number of people had seen the plans, but since the town had few zoning ordinances there was no long approval process. No public meetings where petty grudges would waste hours and amount to nothing. No private meetings where palms would be greased and deals made. The developer's plans called for preserving most of the trees, to remove them would be a lengthy and expensive task. Lawns were fitted in where the land was clear.

Johnny and Bobby, a couple of the town's boys with particularly active imaginations, had the time of their lives playing among the half-dug basements of the tyrant's dungeons, the sleeping hulks of dragon bulldozers, and trebuchets of half-built houses. The construction crews didn't take long turning the Bunsen ancestral home into a nice, new, modern subdivision called Bridle Hill. Before long, the "McMansions", as some of the older and more ornery townsfolk called them, were being advertised for sale in the city. Few in town could have afforded one of these modern luxury homes and those that could were already happy with the homes they had. Only a few people in town even paid much attention when a new resident moved in, as Bridle Hill was set off from the rest of the town by its placement on the other side of the park at the crossroads and most stores and homes were on the other side. Mr. and Mrs. Magnus did try their best to welcome the new residents with cookies or flowers and Mrs. Parker did her best to meet them and glean what she could about their lives from a short conversation when they came into town shopping or walking around.

People normally greeted each other in this town and when they saw a new resident they were warm and cordial. This gave the new residents a nice home-town feeling for Boudton and they all enjoyed living there. "Off the beaten path" was the worst compliment it got.

The months passed and it seemed as if everything would be fine. Just fine the way it was, the way it had been.

CHAPTER TWO

TOWN MEETING

The Boudton town meeting was held annually on March 20. Most of the time, it coincided with the vernal equinox. People were ready to be done with winter; they could see the early flowers peeking up from the ground after their season's rest. The meeting had been held in the same place for the last 150 years - in the fire hall. Most called it the fire hall, some called it the garage at the fire station. The three large bays that would normally house the town's fire trucks would instead be filled with chairs brought from all over town. Most chairs would be of the standard folding variety. There were hard, cold, metal ones; soft, unstable plastic ones; and the occasional padded type, often purchased by a grandchild for a grandparent just for this event.

Quite a few people and families would bring their own chairs, and many were brought by the different groups in town. The chairs brought over by the students of the Catholic school at St. Albinus were filled in by those regular attendees of the attached church. The Elks Club chairs were, more often than not, sat upon by the Elks.

Each set of chairs looked different from the others. Some groups put a great deal of work into making sure their chairs were unique. Oftentimes one of the groups would fire another volley in the "great chair war". One year the dairy farmers showed up with wooden barrels to sit upon. A favorite reminiscence of the book club was the time they talked the high school glee club and attending athletes to go around to each of their homes and collect their living room easy chairs and bring them to the meeting. The line of high, winged-back armchairs caused the Elks to wish they'd put tassels on *their* recently purchased chairs. Even the unofficially affiliated groups would add a bit of flavor, like the time the customers of the Empty Pump recreated their favorite establishment: cinder blocks and planks for a bar, stools and beer nuts; no liquor though, the sobriety rules were strictly enforced at the meetings.

The crowd arrived slowly, as usual, greeting their friends and neighbors, even if this were the one time of the year when they saw them. Some arrived annoyingly early, like Mrs. Parker, who felt it was her job to see everything there was to see in the town. Her advice on how best to pull the trucks out of their bays seemed quite unnecessary to the volunteer firefighters who had done it dozens of times before.

The front few rows of chairs, set up by the members of the fire department were filled by the aged, the more interested, or those with the most business before the town council.

Much of the town waited with curious eyes to see how many of the new arrivals from Bridle Hill would be there. To their surprise, almost all of them had shown up, but without their own chairs. They were taking up most of the front rows. This surprised the realtor, Mr. Tarrole, who was sure he had mentioned the unusual custom of bringing your own seats, and even remembered a few specific instances when he had regaled the nascent Boudtonites with a particularly funny anecdote regarding the chair war. Mrs. Parker managed to shoo away a few newcomers from some of the seats she was saving in the very front, but some of the older folks who usually had seats up front had to wait until the Elks brought some extra chairs from next door.

The greeting, reminiscing, and stories from the previous year were heartily passed around until the clock neared seven. Most people had found their seats, made faux insults about others' seats and generally settled down when the door above the bay creaked open. It made a particularly annoying sound. A sound of metal scraping on concrete that seemed to be at just the right frequency to reverberate around the room. It was the unmistakable signal that the meeting would soon start. Mrs. Parker shot a dirty look at the fire chief who, each and every year, had assured her he'd have the door fixed by the next year's meeting.

The mayor, Mr. Jack Doien was always punctual. His neighbor used him as an alarm clock of sorts. When Mr. Doien closed his car door and drove to work, his neighbor knew it was exactly eight-fifteen and time for him to get ready to leave as well. The mayor was especially punctual when it came to town meetings. He would start walking down the stairs at six fifty-eight, greet the rest of the town council on the make-shift platform at one minute 'til and promptly gavel the meeting to order at seven o'clock sharp. The talking would simmer down, the chair-jeering would cease and Robert would rule with order, or at least, this town's abbreviated version of it. A short speech about the last year would be read.

The mayor would proudly announce births, solemnly remember deaths and generally catch everyone up on important events. Especially for the benefit of those who rarely paid attention to anything beyond their own lives. A brief mention and welcome was made to the new arrivals, hailing those of Bridle Hill and those who had moved in to other parts of town. The secretary of the council, who this year was the local plumber, Mr. Namari, read the previous meeting's minutes, only closely attended by old Claude Wardor, Esq. listening for any mistakes. Few ever questioned Mr. Wardor's objections when he had them. They were far more than often right and as he had been the lawyer for most everybody in town, he had first-hand knowledge of most of the legal happenings. The mayor would again take to the lectern and recap the council actions over the previous year.

The interesting part to the rest of the town was the new business. While the majority of the issues brought before the town council were serious and well thought out, there would be the occasional attempt at humor by suggesting Ms. Tonsor's current hairdo be proclaimed a disaster area or national treasure, depending on the outcome of her latest experiment.

Most people felt few things needed to be changed about the town. The taxes were low because the town spending was low, and that's how people liked it. Suggestions of where a new traffic light or stop sign might be needed were

rare. Land-use and zoning were hardly ever
discussed. All the land in the town was owned by
someone and it generally stayed the way it had
been; farmers had their farmland, homeowners
had their homes, apartment dwellers rented
from the apartment owners, offices were leased
by businessmen, and stores were owned by the
retail establishments. Only when buildings were
owned by people outside the community did
there seem to be any trouble.

A few years ago when the Tomanaki Corporation
tried buying up various storefront properties
there was a problem. The large corporation
thought they would have their new store set up
easily; they'd done it many times before and in
many different places. They needed to combine a
number of the current storefronts to make their
larger establishment. But a couple of the existing
owners did not want to sell. The corporation
lawyers went to the town council asking that the
current owners be made to sell. The increased
tax revenue that the larger store would bring
into the town coffers was surely a good enough
reason to require the current owners to sell, and
they were offering a good price. No one on the
council seemed to think that one larger store
would be better than the current ones - even if
some of the stores were empty at the moment.
The corporate lawyers huffed and puffed but

eventually went someplace else. Generally, the town council had little to do. Things stayed much the way they always had been. People were free to change their own property as they wished, within reason. Keeping the peace in this peaceful town was not a hard job.

But this time when the call for new business before the council came there were quite a few hands up, and most of those hands were attached to the arms of the new residents of Bridle Hill.

The first was Susan Harrigan, a handsome woman in her mid-thirties. Her face, like her crisp, gray suit, was entirely business-like. The word around town was that she was the youngest senior vice-president at the Hamilton Federated Bank. Her no-nonsense manner gave credence to the story. The mayor pointed to her and motioned with an uplifting hand gesture, she rose and spoke:

"The environment is continually besieged by non-recycled material. Every day thousands of empty bottles are introduced into the metropolitan waste stream. The very water that brings us life is bottled up in plastic containers that are choking the planet. We should all be ashamed of ourselves for not more diligently addressing the problem. I therefore, demand the council institute a five-cents-per-bottle surcharge on all beverages sold in our town to fund the establishment of a mandatory recycling program."

A few of the old-timers bristled at the mention of "our town" by such a new-comer. This was an area where pedigree was measured in generations, not in weeks, months, or even years. The word "demand" hardly sang to anyone's ears either. A general murmur was heard throughout the hall, with many looking over at the grocery store owner, Mr. Verde, and to Mr. and Mrs. Viix who ran the convenience store out by the highway. With a broad look at the room and a smug, self-assured look on her face Ms. Harrigan sat down.

Mr. Namari looked at her unbelievingly for a moment and then called out, "Motion presented, do I hear a second?" A short gap of silence passed before another member of the new Bridle Hill development called out, "Seconded." Mr. Namari with his pen held up, looked pleadingly at the mayor. A moment's questioning glance was followed by a nod of understanding. He rose and said, "Since we have so many new faces here tonight, please state your name if you are unknown to the secretary so that our records

will be complete. Your name, mam?" Again Ms. Harrigan stood.
"My name is *Ms.* Susan Harrigan, and I am not a *madam.*"
"Thank you, *Ms.* Harrigan. And you, sir?" the mayor addressed the man who had seconded the motion. Looking rather sheepish at having been called out, the man replied, "Frank Wattle". The mayor thanked them for their understanding and the meeting proceeded.

A distinguished-looking man with gray hair at the temples and a tan, healthy face stood up and said, "I propose the great town of Boudton adopt the Meadow Cranesbill as the official town flower. A modest expenditure to plant these beautiful flowers all around town, out on the approach roads near the town signs and in the park would add a distinctive look and give us all something we can be proud of."

Ms. Harrigan quickly stood and seconded the proposal. Mrs. Swanson, the baker from the local grocery store, raised her hand, stood up and said:

"I would like to speak against this proposal. We don't need an official flower or official anything else to feel proud of this town. External symbols create a false pride, a manufactured pride. Real pride comes from inside. It comes from how we act towards ourselves and our neighbors, only empty pride will be bought with contrived items. And besides, on a factual note, first it's money spent on flowers and then someone thinks the town sign isn't fancy enough next to these beautiful flowers, so we have to spend more money on a nicer sign. Then, next thing you know, the soil in the park isn't right for these flowers or the drainage or whatever and they'll be a proposal to rebuild the whole village square and then we'll need more flowers out by the new sign and then a better sign after that. And that, my friends, is how you send a village to the poor house. The taxes to pay for this will have to come from somewhere and that somewhere is our pockets. Pretty soon people will start having trouble paying these taxes and the next thing you know there's no one left in town to pay them. I say this is a road that will lead to ruin. Before long someone will propose that everybody on Main Street has to paint their store or house with the same color scheme."

She sat down abruptly with her arms folded and a disgusted look on her face. Around this same time, an arm that was raised came down slowly as if hoping no one would notice.

Mr. Namari had furiously been making notes

during the preceding rant and looked up to see if Mrs. Swanson was done. Seeing no one standing he flipped the page and looked expectantly over the crowd.

The next hand called on for new business stood up. "Hello everyone, I'm Roger Van Lailt and my proposal is something I'm sure we'll all agree on. The dangers introduced by cars in our downtown area are quite serious. I can't tell you how many times I've seen someone, usually one of these precious small children, almost get run over by a car. The havoc these machines can wreak on this beautiful town is enormous. Not to mention the noise and pollution. I propose a ban on all motorized vehicles in the downtown area."

Another wave of murmurings swept through the high-ceilinged hall. Before Mr. Namari could ask for a second, a woman rose up in the back and burst forth thusly:

"All motorized traffic, are you insane? Would that also include my mother who relies on a gogo cart to do her shopping? You would have her be imprisoned in her house?" Her voice crept up higher with each word. Mr. Van Lailt looked aback.
"No, mam. I'm sure there's a service that would help her with shopping and the like." The

objector's face got redder and she replied, "Service?! You would have the woman who quite proudly, and almost single–handedly, I might add, held this town together during World War II when half the town was dying overseas and the other half dealing with all the wartime restrictions, to rely on some *service* to do her shopping? Do you realize the art only she has perfected?" At this point she nodded proudly at her mother next to her, sitting in the gogo cart, with its hand-painted flames on the side. "...of picking the perfect melon by its smell? Or the correct snap a green bean needs to have to assure it's inclusion in her four-bean salad? Perhaps you'll say next she could always go out to the super-mart in Conville where they truck, train, or ship the fruits and veggies in from who knows where? I do not second this motion!"

Mr. Van Lailt was going to attempt a response when Mr. Chloris rose to say, "I also think this is a bad idea. I would say eighty percent of my flower shop business is from people stopping by on their drive home from work. Putting me and three, even, three and a half employees - Jimmy works part-time doing deliveries - out of work because someone doesn't like cars in town, on the road - where they belong I might add, is a ludicrous idea. As far as I know, no one has been hit by a vehicle in town, in like, forever.

Excluding Mr. Dips, of course, but that was only because he was seeing what it was like to be a dog for a day and was chasing cars and actually caught one. Although I don't think Mr. Namari's rear bumper was any the worse for wear." A few people chuckled at the memory of one of Mr. Dips' more amusing antics. Mr. Chloris continued, "I consider this a personal attack against my livelihood, and I strongly suggest the council vote against any such action."

The council secretary once again looked puzzled as he said, "Objections so noted - do I hear a second?" Ms. Harrigan immediately popped up from her chair and said, "I second that motion." And with a nod to a slightly embarrassed Mr. Van Lailt, she sat down. The call for new business once again rang out and another hand picked.

"Hi, my name is Grace Wattle and I would like to propose a ban on tree cutting within the village limits. I understand the actual village limits extend out quite a ways so we could protect a great many trees. As we all know trees provide oxygen for the air we breathe and perform water filtration duties, not to mention their beauty. There are trees around here that have been nurturing the earth for hundreds of years, far older than any of us and I think we owe a duty to the earth to help protect these wonderful guardians of our planet." With this, the middle-aged woman with a fevered continence sat down. Mr. Namari didn't even look up as he asked for a second. Again the quick-standing Ms. Harrigan stood up to second the motion.

Other new business was proposed, but nothing that interested more than a few people. Proposals to make slight modifications to existing rules, and a suggestion that a rule concerning wooden-spoke vehicles be removed rounded out the meeting. At this point Mr. Thale the town comedian, self-proclaimed, rose to make a proposal.

"Ladies and gentlemen of the council, the gravity of my proposal is great, but one I feel we can all, no we *must*, consider. The new residents in Bridle Hill having shown themselves to be cut from a different cloth than the rest of the town, I hereby propose redrawing the town map to specifically carve out the new development which I'm sure will prove to be nothing but a boil on the butt of our fair town. Yes, in time these interlopers will prove to be a festering, turgid boil on our behinds, begging for a lancing like a bloated..."

"That will be quite enough Mr. Thale",

Interrupted the mayor. "This town meeting will not be used as a place for your personal mirth and insulting our new neighbors. If you were half the man I think you are, you'd apologize, but since I know you're not I won't even suggest it. As this concludes the new business portion of the meeting, I now call a thirty minute recess before we make the announcement of resolutions concerning old business."

For the next half-hour people milled about, caught up on stale gossip, smoked in the fire training room, or checked out any new equipment they hadn't seen yet. The new residents huddled off by themselves to congratulate each other on their wonderful proposals or talk about how nice it will be once those proposals were put in place. The members of the town council organized the new proposals and made sure the mayor's list of old business was complete and accurate. After twenty-nine minutes and thirty seconds the mayor rose from his spot and held the gavel high in hand and waited. The people noticed the signal and took their seats. Right at the thirty-minute mark the wooden hammer came down with a crack and the meeting resumed.

"Now to old business", the mayor declared. "On Mrs. Johnson's proposal to increase the length of the yellow signal at the intersection of maple and pine; the council agrees and has made a request to the state traffic control board to implement the change." Mrs. Johnson got a few pats on the back and a number of hear-hears from scattered friends around the room. "On the proposal from Mr. Ballard to change the date of the fall festival by a week: proposal declined by the council. The council would like to add that his presence, and his often prize-winning pumpkin pie, will be missed, but that the timing of his cousin's distant wedding is not cause enough to change the date of a date that hasn't been changed in one hundred and fifty-two years." A smile from the mayor and a nod of understanding from Mr. Ballard meant there were no hard feelings. "As that concludes the old business, I think this meeting has come to an end." Before the mayor could reach the gavel, a hand went up and a call of "point of order, Mr. Mayor" was heard. The mayor spotted the caller and said, "Yes, Mr. Gantt isn't it?" "Yes, Ray Gantt, your honor. I'd like to know, when we will have approval on the proposals that have been introduced today?" The mayor took a breath and patiently explained, "The council's decision will be heard at the next town meeting, the discussions and debates will take place a number of times between now and then, please see the schedule posted at the town office for the particular time and location."

Mr. Gantt seemed taken aback. "A year?! We have to wait a whole year? I find that amazing, isn't there some sort of emergency protocol that we can use?"

"Yes, the council will hear emergency resolutions at any time. Do you have an emergency?"

"Well, in that case, I would like to submit that all of the proposals submitted this evening be considered on an emergency basis."

"But, Mr. Gantt, none of the proposals this evening were of an emergency nature."

"I understand, but to move the process along more quickly, couldn't we use the emergency procedures?"

"No, Mr. Gantt, we couldn't. Emergency procedures are exactly that, for emergencies. Taking the time to carefully consider every proposal is an important job. *Hasty decisions bare poor actions.* I believe one of the town founders said that. Now, unless there are any true emergencies I declare this meeting adjourned. For those that wish to imbibe, I understand the tradition of first round on Mr. Blane is still in force, is that right Mr. Blane?" A big thumbs-up from the incessantly cheerful bar owner brought a 'prost', 'kanpai', and 'zdorovye' from a number of Empty Pump fans around the room and a broad grin from Mr. Dips.

Everyone got up to take care of their chairs and return the fire station to its natural order. The residents of Bridle Hill left without talking with anyone. Sulky and petulant, the line of new residents snaked their way back to Mr. Gantt's tiki-torch lined patio. There under the branches and leaves of old oaks with a sprinkling of stars from above, they drank mai tais and talked about how backwards this town seemed to be.

The old townsfolk cleaned up from the meeting, paying the younger helpers with ice cream coupons or "get out of homework free" passes as they chose. Most people of the town went home to help finish homework, clean up from dinner, and relax in front of the TV or sleep. A few took advantage of Mr. Blane's offer of a free drink at the Empty Pump and they played darts, shot pool, or just talked. There were conversations about sports, the weather, and the new waitress over at the Route 22 diner.

Mr. Dips was explaining the difference between a "brougham" and a "landau" to young Ralph Meads who was enjoying his first time in the Empty Pump since he got the OK from his father. Which came a few years after his legal coming of age, as young Ralph would repeatedly point out. Mrs. Dorchester was at a table with the Flemish twins, home from college, who were adamantly explaining to their favorite aunt how French Impressionism changed the world of art. Their conversation was drowned out every now and then by boisterous laughter coming from the bar as someone would fail trying to win an extra free drink besting one of Mr. Blane's bar bets.

It was a weeknight and no one stayed very late. Mr. Blane closed up early. He walked Mr. Dips home, a comforting ritual, the old lush rarely needed any real help, but they both felt satisfied that the day was done when they said goodnight to each other. Mr. Dips would watch the proprietor walk down the street and around the corner before heading into his empty house to fall asleep in his clothes. Mr. Blane would go home to his wife, who always waited up. She worked at the hair salon in town. It was said that between the two of them, they didn't *not* know everything about everyone in town. As neither one of them started work until noon, their nightly ritual of a very late dinner and an hour of talk over their pillows suited them well. As they fell off to sleep, their hands would automatically clasp together. Hands, body, and hearts, tucked in for the night.

CHAPTER THREE

CARS

Roger Van Lailt's commute was rather long. As the chief customer relations manager at the Luxtam Corporation his days were spent being a soother of irascible customers. Each of these days was sandwiched between two forty-five minute layers of driving alone. It was time alone in the morning to prepare for the stress of "oiling the squeaky wheels", and again at night a time of de-stressing from the day's emotionally arduous tasks.

When a customer-complaint call got escalated far enough, he would take over and make things right. His skill at changing irate customers, bent on reducing the company to rubble into lifelong, loyal advocates of the Luxtam family of businesses were legend. He had never failed to assuage the wrath of a returner of defective or unwanted merchandise. He had always managed to concoct just the right plan to take an unhappy consumer and transform him into a fan of "Luxy", the all-too-cute mascot of the numerous Luxtam businesses. He would pander when needed, encourage when called for, or even scold if he thought that would elicit the response he wanted. He would switch sides mid-conversation so tactfully, that the focus of his talents would never notice. From initial stating of the company policies, to complete agreement that "the corporate world is out to get us", he would dance with the terms, seduce the small print and charm the hold-harmless clauses into willing submission, all for the satisfaction of the customer.

Only once in the last ten years did a situation go to official arbitration. The errant customer was railing about injustice and threatening global cataclysm if he were not satisfied. He never allowed Roger to talk, but insisted wholeheartedly on an arbitration meeting. This caused quite a stir around the office, as any unique event will. On the day of the meeting Mr. Roger Van Lailt, resplendent in a freshly laundered suit, politely met the customer at the door and walked him through the lobby to the main conference room. Knowing that offering the upset customer a coffee or other hospitality would only allow him to lash out with charges of bribery or worse, Roger sat quietly, not saying a word except to explain that they were waiting on the arbitrator, a certain retired Judge Albight. He sat rather docilely, watching the moves of his target, gauging different approaches and waiting for opportunities to achieve his goal: a happy, returning customer and an unblemished record.

The arbitrator arrived, cold and steely, ready to seed out justice to the malevolent and wisdom to the aggrieved. Relishing the position as both judge and jury and holding his head as if his years as a member of the bar were so many leaves in a laurel crown, he was willing to spank either of these parties if they didn't show deference to his personal position or the rules of what he thought of as *his* game.

A small group of Luxtam employees gathered near the conference room waiting for a verdict on the infallibility of "their man". A few rounds of wagering took place between those in the office that wanted to see their boss put down and humiliated, and those certain of his escape from a meal of humble pie.

The meeting lasted two hours. At its conclusion, all were left in a speechless awe. Those who dreamed of weeks, months or even years of teasing and practical joke-playing were despondent. Those who hoped for a best-case win of a former customer who didn't take out ads in the local paper excoriating the company for foul business practices were amazed. The three men came out of the conference room, laughing and joking as if they were old army buddies who hadn't seen each other in years. The erstwhile destroyer of the Luxtam world was accompanied off to the sales department by a senior manager to place his largest order yet and the granite judge was shown to the human resources department to prepare for a job as a Luxtam corporation legal advisor.

But victories such as these were not without cost. Each angry call produced a gray hair. Every unhappy customer seemed to sprout an irritating polyp in Roger's colon. The anger of the unsatisfied clients washed around his face leaving wrinkles, wrinkles that the inevitable satisfaction would never completely smooth out. All the harsh words directed at him and the company he took personal pride in pushed into his veins and distended them, and raised his blood pressure to unsafe levels. The stress of departmental goal-seeking meetings pulled and pushed on his muscles until they were a knotted mass of pain. The combined weight of his numerous managers' expectations bore down upon him in nearly unbearable ways.

But he had his commute. His drive-time therapy, as he called it. It was when he replaced all the complicated situations and vitriolic speech with the simpler actions of changing lanes and staying within four miles-an-hour of the posted speed limit. There would be music on the radio and calm in the empty car. The inexplicable vacillations of human emotions and sensibilities were swapped out, for a time, with the orderly flow of traffic. Incomprehensible lines of thought were gone and the obvious, predictable lines of the highway kept everyone rational. The complicated warranties, poorly designed forms, and dense, legal small print were nowhere to be seen. Only the simplicity of driving remained. Clearly posted speed limit signs and an accurate speedometer soothed his racing heart. A purple smear of red and blue flashing lights in the rear-view mirror did not send him into a panic. He knew it was someone else, not him, who would be pulled over and submitted to humiliation. The traffic lights of the towns along the way let him know when to go and when to stop. He didn't have to think about which way to go, the signs were clear and he knew the way well. He did not have to out-think, re-think, or around-think to accomplish his goal. He only had to go the way he knew. Since he moved from the suburbs to Boudton, and the fashionable Bridle Hill development at that, over a year ago, it was the same way every time.

As he got close to Boudton he was nearly calm, most of the day's angst left next to friendly mile markers and comforting guardrails. The clouds in the distance, wet and heavy, held no menace. Instead they held the promise of water for his chrysanthemums, life for his lawn and a contribution to another ring of growth for his trees. The friendly visage of his new hometown greeted him over the hill. A short drive through the outskirts to the town park and he would be home. He would be home to relax and look at his beautifully landscaped grounds.

Turning into the Bridle Hill entrance gave an even greater sense of calm. Here was home, peace, and serenity. The rain was falling generously. "I'll get the mail tomorrow morning", he thought, passing his barn-shaped mailbox complete with rooster wind vane and white crossbeam highlights as he pulled up the drive. The garage door opened obediently and his car slowly slid to a halt in the spacious garage. Yard tools neatly lined the walls like slim, attentive soldiers, ready and waiting for the order to attack the weeds and repel the constant invasion of nature's disorder. His faithful gendarmes, cohorts, and compatriots bonded by the esprit de corps of creating order and beauty from the unruly masses of bushes and shrubs stood always at the ready. A wave of joy swept over him, not enough to undo all the pain of the day, but enough to keep him going. The joy at his control and mastery of the world around him always kept him going. Through the decidedly un-muddy mudroom, past the pristine kitchen, keeping his sight indoors, because today he wanted to go upstairs to his master bedroom suite, change into shorts and a tee shirt and only then step out onto the redwood balcony and gaze at his handiwork. He knew how it would look, his decorative trees ringed with seasonal flowers, his straight, regimented rows of boxwoods and shrubs impeccably trimmed; waiting for nothing more than to give pleasure to his eyes. He knew what his koi pond would look like, its surface dancing with the summer rain twisting the reflections of the brightly colored gold, black, and white fish beneath. He could almost feel them tucked under the pads of his Nymphaeaceae, their flowers sprouting tall and proud. He was awaiting the sound of the stream; the hand-made, *his hands made*, stream. He knew it would be swollen with rainwater, babbling around the bends and under the arched bridge to the lower pond. He wouldn't be able to see it, but he knew the water would be pumped and aerated back up to the main pond to refresh and invigorate his expensive fish pets.

As he got out of his suit, stripping off the uniform of his daytime labor, he noticed an unusual sound. "The rain seems louder than normal," was his passing thought as he pulled back the curtains and slid open the large glass door, stickered with flowers to keep hapless birds from crashing into it. The sight that met him was not one of placid calmness and an orderly universe. Instead it was an assault on every one of his senses.

His ears were hammered with the sound of the rain, not slapping against the surface of the ponds, or dancing merrily on the planks of his garden bridge. They were being pounded upon by the sound of angry drops crashing against the rusted metal hulks of dead automobiles. There were dozens of them splashed haphazardly about the yard, covering almost every foot of ground. His eyes ached trying to take in all of the twisted metals, corroded angles and faded fenders. Instead of the sweet petrichor his imagination foretold, his nostrils were invaded with an odiferous violation of oil, grease, rotting leather and burnt rubber. The beautiful Acer Summer Red trees were now nothing more than expensive rugs under the oppressive weight of burned-out husks. Instead of a loving home for the imported koi the upper pond was a gash in the bosom of mother earth with the rear-end of a nineteen seventy-eight country squire station wagon completely filling its depth. The pond's diligently placed rocks were spewed about by the car as if it had been thrown down from the heavens by an angry god. His gorgeous, arched, oriental style bridge had been crushed by a nineteen eighty-four Saab that looked like it had been in any number of crashes prior to this one. A pair of Volkswagen Bugs, one faded yellow, the other in bleached red, laid in cushiony repose upon the boxwoods. He couldn't even see the rhododendrons as they were hidden beneath the bulky expanse of a pickup truck, which itself was completely flattened as if it were pulled mid-stream in its journey to the smelter. The forsythia seemed as garnish for the Mercedes sedan nestled among it fronds, its surface slick and gleaming like a pig at luau being roasted on the beach.

In a near panic Mr. Van Lailt picked up the phone and dialed nine-one-one. A ringing signal was heard, then,

"Nine-One-One, operator number seventeen, please state the nature of your emergency".
"It's my yard. My yard is covered with cars."
"Yes, sir I understand there's been an automobile accident, is anyone hurt?"
"No, not an accident, just cars…uh, everywhere."
"Are you hurt sir?"
"No, I'm fine, but my plants, my bridge, there are cars everywhere."
"I don't understand sir, have you been involved

in a traffic accident?"

"No, but there are cars all over my back yard, they've ruined my pond, crunched my trees, they're everywhere."

"Sir, if this I not an actual emergency, you need to contact your local police."

"It *is* an emergency, it's horrendous, the cars are everywhere!"

"I understand sir, but if there are no bodily injuries, you need to contact your local law enforcement agency."

"But you're not listening to me, there are dozens of cars, they're all over my yard!"

"Sir, abandoned property is not within the prevue of an emergency situation. You'll need to contact your local police."

"But I, but there's..."

"Sir, unless you want me to log this call as a fraudulent use of the emergency response system - we need to clear this line for real emergencies."

"Fine, yes, I'll call them."

"Thank you, sir."

A few moments later, after wrestling with the phonebook, looking under the Ps, almost getting there then dropping the book from the shaking of his hands only to see the number on the front cover, he hastily dialed the number, hoping he could get a hold of someone quickly. The number punched in, the connection made, the gentle purring of the ring on his end indicating the incessant clanging on the other, or perhaps the annoying chirping, twittering sound on the other side impelling someone at the local police department to answer the phone. There was a click, then a pause, and a languid, but friendly, voice on the other end.

"Boudton police department, Chief Jardem speaking."

"Hello, yes, Chief Jardem? This is Roger Van Lailt, there are cars everywhere!"

"Yes, yes there are. The roads are full of them. How can I help you now?"

"No, yes, I know there are cars on the road, but now there are cars in my yard!"

"Cars in your yard, huh? Well, are you having a party?"

"No, I'm not having a party; someone has put cars all over my yard."

"Well, can you describe them?"

"No, I have no idea what they look like; I didn't see them do it."

"You mean the cars put themselves on your yard, no one was driving?"

"I don't know who was driving, I mean they weren't driven on, they'll all derelicts"

"How do you know derelicts put cars on your yard?"

"No, the people aren't derelicts, the cars are!"
"So you know who put them there then."
"No, I have no idea who put them here, they're just here!"
"Just here, huh? Where are these cars?"
"They're in my back yard. All over my landscaping and trees and, and, and, everything!"
"Well, where is your yard?"
"Behind my house obviously."
"And where would your house be?"
"Oh, right. I'm at 1544 Saddle Way."
"Perhaps I'd better send someone over to take a look - hang on, I think officer Voet is over that way. I'll radio him to go take a look."
"Wait, I..."
"Hold on a minute."

In the background he heard a burst of static, then "Chief calling Vlad. Come in, are you there?" There was a click and then the lilting strains of a particularly sappy version of *The Girl from Ipanema* greeted him as hold music.

Chief Jardem radioed to car two and told him there was a possible crazy person or possibly crazy cars or both. The usually calm officer, thrilled to have an actual situation that deserved his attention in this equally calm town, said he'd get right over there.

The agitated Mr. Van Lailt, still trembling from the shock of finding his yard violated by a host of discarded automobiles, was waiting impatiently for the sound of the chief's voice on the other end of the line.

"Are you still there, sir?"

"Yes, yes, of course I'm still here. What are you going to do about all these cars?"

"Officer Voet is on his way to take a look-see."

"A look-see? But what are you going to do?"

"Well, I'm not sure, sir. They're on your land, but you say they aren't your cars?"

"Yes, no, I mean they are not my cars and *yes* they are on my land. My whole back yard is covered with them; in fact there must be hundreds of them."

"Hundreds, huh? And you have no idea how they got there?"

"No, no idea at all. I left for work this morning as usual and everything was fine and beautiful and this afternoon when I got home everything's wrecked. Who's going to get rid of all of these things?"

"Well, it seems to me that if they're on your yard, then they're your cars now, you can get rid of them however you like. You do have insurance, right? I don't know if homeowner's or automobile would be more in line here, but..."

"What? Is that a joke, this is no joking matter, chief. In fact I want you over here right away and

tell me what you're going to do about this, who's going to pay for all this?"
"What kind of cars are they? Maybe you could sell them for a lot of money, maybe this is a good thing."
"A good thing? That's crazy, everything's ruined!"
"Well, I'll certainly come over and take a look. If it's like you say, I can't wait to take a look. I'll be right on my way"
"Yes, you sure will, I mean it's a disaster!"
"Sure, huh? Disaster, huh? Well, we'll see. I'll be over in a few minutes, bye-bye."
"Good-bye."

Old Mrs. Parker loved her radio scanner. Years ago, before her husband died, he bought her a multi-band radio scanner to keep her company while he was away running errands, visiting friends or just out in his shed puttering around. It could receive police, fire and emergency radio traffic from all over the county. It gave her a sense of connection, not just to the wider world, but since his death, to her late husband. It made her feel as if he were still around somewhere, just outside in the yard re-potting a ficus, or down in his shed still fixing up the old vacuum; and while the vacuum was still there, her husband was not. He had left a space behind, in her.

Mrs. Parker was in the kitchen boiling potatoes for her famous twice-baked 'canoes'. The boiling pot's hair of steam was twisting its way to the ceiling, the jars and pots of spices were standing around, heads open, ready to serve up their essence, and the vigilant scanner was scouring the airwaves for trouble. Between its buzzing and static she heard of traffic pullovers on the highway, jokes from the state troopers and training calls from the Conville volunteer fire company. What she heard today, however, was Chief Jardem. She heard him explain that there were some strange goings-on over at Bridle Hill. This piqued her attention, as it would have most of the other townsfolk after the display the new people had put on at the town meeting. As this was a bit of exciting local news, she hesitated only slightly before carefully putting down her paring knife and calling her daughter-in-law to tell her what she had heard.

She was careful these days to only call when something *real* was happening. Over the years she had been admonished for calling up when she heard about a flat tire on the interstate, or when the Conville fire chief radioed the station that the diner up on route 24 had a special on cherry pie. But this was real news in their town and she was sure that *that woman who married my son* would appreciate knowing. Especially as it had to do with the new housing development and everyone in town was keen on knowing news about that. While Mrs. Parker was telling, Diane; that was her real name, her external name, as opposed to the one she used in her head, Diane's son Johnny was in the next room to his mother, staring at a video game on the TV, half bored, but still intent on saving the world from an invasion of zombies. He managed to pick up the words *police, lots of cars,* and *Bridle Hill* from his mother's half of the conversation. This was enough to prick up the boy's ears and make him take interest. In a matter of moments he was off, with a brief "going to play" to his mother, still on the phone, and he was out, headed towards his friend Bobby's house. After a quick explanation to his friend, the boys were off in search of adventure, or at least to see what they were sure was the remnants of an impressive car crash. Through a few well-chosen back yards, across a winding brook, past the old mill, that now housed the Boudton professional building; they came to the village park. They stopped for just a minute to watch the town drunk, Mr. Dips, who was having a conversation with the roses on the south end of the park.

A quick run across Main Street and they were in Bridle Hill. They weren't sure which way to go until they saw Officer Voet's cruiser turn right and head around the loop. Knowing the area well, even before the houses were there, they plotted the best path through the houses and trees; being careful to avoid the Clupis place and their notoriously noisy dogs, not to mention their attendant mess. Approaching from the rear of the property they had no problem seeing the carnage of Mr. Van Lailt's yard through the trees as they got close; unlike Officer Voet who had just pulled up in the front.

Officer Vlad, as pretty much everyone called him, saw no cars as he slowed into the driveway. The lawn looked neat and crisp, all the edges clear and sharp, the flowers arranged in tidy rows. And as he was upwind, the only smell he noticed was that of grasses, trees, and rain drying on the pavement. He walked up to the large front door, pushed an elaborately adorned button and heard the notes of *Westminster Quarters* inside. After puzzling for a moment on the choice of a clock-sound announcing a visitor, the door was yanked open by a frazzled-looking Roger Van Lailt. Officer Vlad's attempt at opening pleasantries were cut short by Mr. Van Lailt insisting that the officer see the damage and demanding to know what was going to be done about it. The officer was led to the back deck and shown the yard. It seemed like a scene from a disaster movie. *Herbie Rides from the Grave*, Officer Vlad chuckled inwardly as the target of the joke was working himself into a froth while listing the damage done to his beloved, previously manicured now ex-garden of Eden.

Officer Vlad took out his pad and began making notes on the, he'd counted thirty-six so far, twice-abandoned cars. They were foreign and domestic, sedans and pickups, new and old. There was even one just like the first car he ever owned, although the one planted in the middle of Mr. Van Lailt's petunia patch was a different color and had the "landau" roof. He begun walking among them, the cars looking like a sculpture garden for Mad Max rejects or failed attempts from the auto shop repair school over in Conville. Checking the ground carefully, he looked to see how the cars were actually placed here. He couldn't tell, initially, how they were placed so quickly and apparently without anyone noticing. With more than two dozen cars being towed around the neighborhood, he would have thought someone would have seen or heard something. He saw tracks: the double, rear-wheeled kind one would expect on a tow truck. No big mystery then, he thought. He followed the tracks out the back of the yard, up a small hill at the rear where they were deeper and more heavily rutted. Following the ruts a bit further, he saw they met up with the old fire road that ran alongside the development. He made a note to check where the fire road connected to Main Street or, more than likely, connected to route 7 , out where it's called Steadman's road. He headed back to the house.

Chief Jardem arrived a few minutes later. He got out of his car and looked around. He saw nothing out of the ordinary. A neat yard surrounding a neat house was all there was. Deciding to look around a bit before having to deal with Mr. Van *do-something-about-it* Lailt, he went around the side of the house. He saw Johnny and Bobby peeking over the hedge that sided the yard, as they'd moved up closer to the house to get a better view. The chief decided to play a little trick on them, so he crept up slowly. "Hands in the air!" he said briskly, but smiled broadly so the boys wouldn't be too shocked. They spun around wildly with panic on their faces until they saw who it was and how he was smiling. Johnny said,
"Holy cow chief, that's not funny"
"Sure it was, to me. What are you two doing sneaking around here?"
"I heard grandma Parker tell mom there was something going on here, something about a big car accident, but we didn't expect anything like

this!"
"Did you boys see anything?"
"Na, we just got here a minute ago, we missed everything."
"Ok, you boys be careful, and you shouldn't be trespassing around here, there are plenty of other places you can play."
"OK, chief."
The boys walked sheepishly, but with a mischievous look in their eyes, back towards town.

Stepping through the gate beside the hedges, the chief finally got a good look at the scene. And it was quite indeed a scene. He thought it looked like the God of Abandoned Cars threw up his entire lunch of Detroit Detritus right in this guy's back yard. They were all angled and piled up in preposterous ways. Someone not only took the time to bring near-on thirty cars to this man's back yard, but took the time and effort to arrange them with an artistic flair. He saw officer Voet talking with the homeowner as the latter was gesticulating wildly and spreading his arms indicating the expanse of the tragedy he was confronted with. The chief let out a sigh, took a breath and walked up to the men. His presence was caught by the attention of the transgressed homeowner.

"Ah, chief, it's about time you got here. What's being done about this?"

"Well, let's go down to the station and we'll take your statement, see what officer Voet has come up with, and we'll begin the investigation."

"Why do I have to go to the station, the people who did this should be down there?"

"You're implying again that you know who did this."

"No, I don't know who did this, why do you keep saying that?"

"You're the one who keeps acting as if you know who it was - we've barely started our investigation."

"Well, I do know who *I'd* start with. I bet this all has to do with the town meeting last month. When I made the suggestion of restricting traffic in the downtown region to pedestrians only - a few people got upset. You saw the reaction, and you saw who protested the most; that flower shop guy, he was awfully hot when he thought that would mean less business for him."

"Well, it's interesting you would say that, yes I saw his reaction. I also noticed hardly anyone else was very interested in that idea."

"Fine, yes, this whole town is filled with troglodytic Neanderthals."

"Well, I don't know about that, and I don't think too many cavemen drove cars."

"You know what I mean. But you make sure you

check with that flower shop guy, I'm sure he had something to do with this, he was awfully violent about it."

"If I recall correctly, all he did was talk about how bad an idea he thought it was. Did he threaten you in some way?"

"Uh, no, he didn't, but he was very angry. And he looked mean."

"Well, I'm sorry Mr. Van Lailt, but looking mean and being angry is not a crime. Before you go too far with this, accusing people and such, I should probably tell you that I know Mr. Chloris, the flower shop guy as you call him. I know him to be quite the pacifist. He's one of the gentlest souls you'll ever meet. He's really not the type to do something like this. And before you say it, he is also not the type to have anyone else do it for him. I also happen to know he's been on a business trip in South America for the past couple of weeks trying to find a Zephyr Bubble, or something like that. I really don't think he's the culprit here."

"Ok, ok, it's not him, but it had to be someone. Cars just don't fall out of the sky and land in people's back yards, you know. I demand action on this! I'll make your lives very difficult if you don't find out who did this and throw them in jail for a long, long time!"

At this point, office Voet spoke up.

"Mr. Van Lailt, I don't wish to be rude, but Mrs.

Swanson over at the bakery counter told me you
were in customer relations or something like
that, is this the same way you treat your
customers? Perhaps there's a disgruntled
customer that has it out for you."
"I, well, no, I don't treat my customers like this.
You're not my customers, but this *is* my yard
and my property. I've been violated and I
completely expect something to be done about
it! Who's going to pay for all the damage, how
am I supposed to get all these cars out of here?"
"I'm sure we can find someone with a tow truck,
or", spinning his head around to look at all the
cars, "two maybe, to have all these cars removed.
Maybe one of those people that take cars away
for free will do it and not charge you. Or maybe
a place that pays for old cars - it might be worth
something to them." said officer Voet.
"Well, maybe, but still, all my plants and flowers
and my bridge, look at my bridge!"
"Well, that is a shame", the chief said, "Let's get
you down to the station so we can fill out all the
proper reports and see if we can't find out who's
behind this."
"Ok, ok fine, fine."
"Vlad, go around and make a list of all the VINs
on these things, maybe we can find out where
they came from."
"Will do, chief."

The chief went back to the station and began filling out the forms required and took a complete statement from Mr. Roger Van Lailt. Who was practically apoplectic by the time they were done, thinking of all the destruction, thinking of the violation, and seriously thinking about moving back to the suburbs he'd come from, now that his piece of paradise had been polluted with the corpses of ancient automobiles.

Johnny and Bobby didn't head back to town and home. They had a blast playing around on the numerous wrecks, avoiding the grass of boiling lava, the evil Dr. Mercedes with his twisted and scarred German henchmen. They only narrowly escaped from the giant weeping willow tree that was a monster junk yard dog. Officer Vlad eventually shooed them away and told them to get home as it was getting dark.

The officer finished writing down all the Vehicle Identification Numbers from the cars and went home to his pleasant wife. They had a tasty dinner of baked chicken with a side order of friendly talk in their quiet home. They went out on the patio afterwards to eat a desert of Mrs. Swanson's apple pie. He'd picked one up on the way home. They watched the sun set behind the trees. No mention was made of trespassing automobiles or irate newcomers. The earlier rain had swept the away day's humidity and the stars shimmered overhead in the clear sky. They slept soundly that night.

CHAPTER FOUR

TREES

Mrs. Grace Wattle slept the sleep of the dead. A double dose of Zolpidem made sure of that. She had taken two of the yellow pills to clear the cares of her day. Her numerous committee positions kept her busy with the cares of the entire world. Most of her days were spent on the computer, sending and answering emails and posts. Between fighting for, or against; wildlife habitat, deforestation, spawning grounds, and pesticide usage, her hours were full and busy. The weight of the world fell on her shoulders and she felt a good night's sleep was her due.

A wonderfully kind and caring woman, most would say, but her family felt otherwise. Her husband had a good job and she, as the only child from a wealthy family, had complete use of her passed parents' trust fund, so between them they had plenty of money. Hiring someone to do the cooking and cleaning was not really the problem. Having someone to take care of the house was a nice advantage, but the time freed up by the "hired help" was not spent by her living life with her family. It was spent trying to heal all the ills of the earth. Mr. Wattle spent his non-working time with their two daughters and spent time on his hobby, stamp collecting, and actually did enjoy spending time with his wife. When he could get her away from the computer or phone, or when she wasn't off on some junket to visit the possible last refuge of the endangered *Gyps indicus* she would more often than not talk about all the problems that weren't being taken care. He liked her nevertheless. But she was rarely there for him or the girls. She would always put their wants and desires behind that of the Pyrenean Brook Salamander or the Blunt Chaff Flower.

She did not normally get up with the rest of her family. Communicating live with her compatriots in other time zones gave her the sense of a dedicated worker for the cause.

That morning started out similarly to most others. She had gotten out of bed and thought, "What a glorious day - it seems so bright this morning." She put on her over-priced, it seemed to the family anyway, fair-trade robe and opened the curtains. It was indeed a beautiful sunny morning. In fact, too sunny. The sun streaked into her window like it never had before. Then she saw why.

The trees in her yard were down. They were on the ground in heaps of tangled branches and leaves. The birch and the oak piled up next to the willow and maple. They were all felled curiously away from the house, their sharpened, bare trunks and stumps pointing like giant arrows toward her family's home. Birds were flitting and squawking in the still-standing trees beyond the yard. She stood in shocked bewilderment at the scene, she could barely think, much less move. Finally, she managed a combination of scream, gargle, and hiss and called out "Fraaaank!" A few moments later she heard footsteps on the stairs and the bedroom door flew open.

Frank said, "Honey, have you seen?"
"Of course I've seen. How could I not? What did you do, how did this happen?"
"I don't know. It must have happened sometime in the night. When the girls and I got up, all the trees were down. Cindi saw it first, it was quite a shock."
"Why didn't you wake me up? What have you done about it - How could you let this happen?"
"I've called the police. Chief Jardem himself said he'd come over. I also called the landscaping service; they'll be over today to take a look and can probably start cleaning up the day after tomorrow. At least we'll have plenty of

firewood."

"Firewood? Is that what this is all about? You know I don't like burning dead trees. How about if I threw your dead Aunt Sally in the fireplace, would you think that was cozy or romantic? Did you do this just because I won't let you burn fires in the house?"

"Now that's uncalled for. I thought you liked Aunt Sally. Anyway, you know I'd never do anything like this. Don't you?"

"I don't know Franklin Wattle. Sometimes I wonder about your motives. You just don't seem to care about the planet."

"I care about this family. Sometimes I wonder about whether…"

"This is a disaster; I have to call the response team immediately."

"I've already called the police; they'll be here any minute."

"Oh, I don't mean those yokels; I need to call *Équipe internationale de réponse pour le désastre environnemental*. They'll want to know all about this right away."

She walked over to the phone and dialed. Mr. Wattle heard her say, "Hello, hello? This is Midnight Foxtrot I have a disaster to report…" He thought he detected a bit of pride in her voice as she started to explain what had happened.

He left the bedroom and went back down to be with his daughters who were busy texting and calling their friends with their exciting, but troubling news. He gave them an I'll-be-outside gesture and went out to the backyard. As he walked around the stumps he slipped on something gooey. Looking down, he saw he'd stepped in some dog poop. He started to curse Mr. Clupis. He stopped when he noticed it didn't look like the abnormally large dog poop left behind by the Clupis dogs. Who had small dogs around here, he wondered. The Clupis dogs were all of monstrous size. Then he looked at the stump nearest him a bit closer. There were teeth marks on the stumps. He saw teeth marks from sharp, little incisors that had scraped, chewed and gnawed on the trees until they had fallen over from their own weight. He realized a beaver had done this.

The realization came with an incredulous set of facts. How could a beaver have taken down all these trees in a single night? How could the trees have fallen without waking everyone in the house, or even the whole neighborhood? And just as odd, why would only these trees have been taken down, just the ones around his house?

One of the questions was answered almost

immediately. A rustle of branches and form of movement caught his attention. A brown figure of fur wiggled under a branch. The beaver moved out of eyesight just as another rustling movement made him look to the right. Another beaver was in the middle of a mass of branches nibbling on a limb, paying attention to nothing else but the job at hand. A scraping sound to his left, just around the corner of the house now called for his attention. He warily peered around the edge of bricks to see three more beavers working steadily to finish up the job they'd started. He'd never seen nor heard of so many beavers being in one area or doing the same job. What could have caused all these beavers to chew down the trees in his yard? He heard a car pull up, so he walked around to the other side of the house, where he saw four more of the busy little rodents dutifully munching on what used to be the yard's pleasant shelter.

Chief Jardem was gazing around with a very puzzled look on his face when Frank walked up and introduced himself. He felt there was no real need for an explanation other than a wide sweeping gesture with his arms. He did say "beavers" and motioned the chief out to the back yard where they both surveyed the incredible scene. They looked at each other and after Frank started to grin, they began smiling at each other.

There was really nothing else to do. The ludicrousness of the situation called for no other action. They beamed with smiles that were equal parts amazement and hilarity. The bright, white stumps sticking up out of the ground like a dozen pencil points was an absurd scene. The various beavers gnawing, grinding, and chewing their way through branches as if they were in the middle of a prime-time nature show cavalcade was too much. They started to laugh. The kind of laugh that they knew they shouldn't be having, but just couldn't help it.

It was as if they were at a royal reception for the queen attended by the most regal ladies and gentlemen of society and some joker next to them had said, "Hey, check out *that* bimbo." Or, as if during a particularly silent and pious part of a church service and a *breaking of wind* bounces off the hard wooden pews to echo around the vaulted ceiling. It was a guilty laugh to be sure. During the laugh a horrible thought struck Mr. Wattle. A dooming thought. Sure enough, as he turned around and looked into the house, his wife was there watching. She did not look happy. If the reddening of her skin was not enough of a clue, the throbbing vein standing out near her temple was more than enough to let Frank know he was in trouble. The two girls behind her had a look that said "sorry", and "we couldn't help it". A reassuring grin from him after their mother had turned and stomped away let them know he didn't blame them.

The chief apologized, admitting it was inappropriate considering the situation. A silent agreement, made with their eyes, also confirmed that this would be one of the funniest stories they would ever tell. It would be a few years before they could tell it with gusto, to be sure, but eventually it would be one of the better ones. The chief went about making notes, trying to figure out how so many beavers ended up in one place, though for him finding out *who* was doing these odd deeds was indeed a much bigger question.

Mr. Wattle went inside, called out from work for that day, took the kids to school and planned on spending the rest of the day placating his wife and trying to get her to understand that some situations call for laughter even though they may seem grim at the time. He hoped that in time she would understand and forgive him.

He found out later in the day part of his wife's consternation was due to the fact that the response team she called, with the hope of this vaulting her to the top of the responsible, concerned savers of the world list, was

uninterested in her "disaster". It seems a few
trees toppled over in a rich lady's comfortable
American home was not worthy of their
attention. There was no massive destruction of
endangered habitat, no wholesale slaughter of a
threatened species, or grave threat to a
downtrodden people. It seems publicity was as
important as the planet to these people and if it
couldn't pull on the heartstrings of a million
people, it wasn't worth their time. She felt they
had treated her like a spoiled child whose ice
cream cone had fallen over and she expected the
world to stop and come to her aid.

The rest of the day was no less frustrating. The
lawn service people came by to see what needed
to be done. When she could tell they too were
having a hard time keeping from laughing she
went inside and let her husband handle things.
She watched them walk around the yard
counting up the trees, figuring how many trips it
would take to haul everything away. She noticed
the part of their conversation when Frank
refused the wood. The bewildered look on their
faces pleased her, as she knew her husband was
defending her desires at the cost of him being
ridiculed. After a few more minutes of Frank
obviously telling them he didn't want the yard
ruined with giant trucks gouging what was left
of his yard, he turned quickly and headed for the

house. She went to the kitchen table to sit down and act unconcerned with what he was doing. "Before I tell them," he begun, "would you rather plant replacement trees yourself, or should I have them do it?" She looked toward him but did not answer right away. "I thought maybe we could plant new ones, you know as a family, and water and feed and watch them grow." She knew it was a kind thought and she would enjoy planting and watching her own trees grow with her family, only she didn't know how to answer and still stay mad. Frank glanced outside to the waiting men but made no words to rush her. "Yes, we'll plant them." was her eventual, brusque response. He went back outside and she watched the animated discussion on how the stumps would have to be ripped out of the ground and new soil brought in to fill in the holes. It looked to her that they were maybe suggesting what kind of trees to put where and what kind of shade they'd get or perhaps flowering trees that would explode with colorful blossoms in the spring.

As they slowly walked around to the front of the house, they discussed the advantages and disadvantages of deciduous and conifer trees. At the edge of the front yard the question of the beavers came up.

"I know it ain't none of my business, but I just gotta ask, what you gonna do with all them beavers?" asked the shorter, greasier of the two men. Frank looked around for a moment, then said,
"Good question, I hadn't really thought much about it until now. I guess I figured they were part of the land and there wasn't much that *could* be done about them."
The taller man with combed hair and a collared shirt with the lawn service company logo on it said, "My cousin out in Conville has a pest removal service. Mostly stuff like mice and ants, but he's pretty good at catching raccoons and bigger things. He's got a great story about the time he chased a big rat, and even though no one really believes him, he tells a great story."
"Thanks, yes. I'll need to get them out of here before they bring down every tree in the neighborhood. He doesn't have to kill them, does he? My wife wouldn't stand for that."
"I'm pretty sure he can catch them and let 'em go somewhere else. Here, I'll give him a call right now and see when he can come over."
"Great, thanks."
The taller man took a few steps away and pulled out his cell phone.
The shorter man said, "Yeah, Brewster's a good guy. My mama Jones went off to visit relations in Ofswitch last year and came back to find her

whole house swarmin' with roaches. I 'spose she
left out some food or somethin'. Brewster came
over and smoked those bad boys out quicker 'n
nothin'. Told me she still hadn't seen a roach,
spider, or fly and it's been goin' on two years
since then."
"Sounds great."
The taller man came back with his hand over the
end of the phone. "He's just down the road a bit
and says he can come over right away if you
like."
"Yes, that'd be wonderful. I'd appreciate it."
He turned around to finish the conversation.
"Make sure 'e tells ya the rat story, it's a hoot. All
ya haf to do is ask about the oddest critter he's
gotten rid of an he'll take it from there." And
with a wink, the greasy man walked off towards
the street and a green truck covered with
paintings of plants. Paintings which looked as if
they were done by first- graders, which in fact
they were. It was part of a project taken on by
the sister of the taller man's first grade class,
during their art module.

Frank Wattle waved goodbye to the men of the
TideeCare Lawn Service and went back inside. He
told his wife the trees would be removed in a few
days and it would hardly cost them anything as
the service could sell the wood since they
weren't going to keep any. She seemed a bit

calmer now. Thoughts of planting new trees and thinking of how proud she would be of them had a calming effect. The news of someone coming to take care of the beavers troubled her a bit. She made it very clear that she had no intention of letting anyone kill the *dear little creatures that were only acting as Mother Nature intended.* Frank assured her he'd be very clear about what was to be done about them and asked if she wanted a nice salad, that he'd be happy to fix her one.

They had a quiet lunch, each absorbed in their own thoughts when they heard a knock on the door. Getting up and saying, "Don't worry, no lethal means, I'll remember", Frank went to answer the door.

He opened the door to reveal a very tall and very thin man standing on the stoop. He had short-cropped hair and one of the broadest, toothiest smiles Frank had ever seen.

"Howdy, Frank, isn't it? My cousin called and said you had a beaver problem. Well, I can sure see that. What the heck happened? I don't think I've ever seen so many trees down from beaver before. Heck, I've never even heard of it before. What'd you guys do, some sort of Indian beaver dance?"

"Uh, no. I have no idea what happened. Last night everything was normal, this morning - no trees and a whole bunch of beaver droppings on the yard."

"Yeah, I can see that. Any idea how many there are?"

"No, I haven't been able to count with any certainty, six that I know of for sure. I've only seen that many at the same time, I don't know if they're running around all over the yard, or if they stay in the same place or what."

"Well, it doesn't really matter. I can take care of them for you. Tell me, are you a married man?"

"Yes, my wife's just inside."

"Would she like a fur coat?"

With a frightened look Frank glanced at the house to make sure she wasn't within hearing range and closed the door behind him as he crowded on to the front stoop with the tall exterminator.

"Oh, Lord no. Don't even think about that. My wife would have us both up before the International Tribunal for Doing Nasty Things to Cute Fuzzy Animals or something like that. She'd kill me. You have to promise me you can remove them without hurting them, it really is terribly important."

"Ok, ok, no problem. I just thought I'd offer. Beaver coats used to be all the rage you know. I prefer not to kill if I don't have to anyway. It's not always as easy, but seems to me to be a whole lot nicer."

"Thanks. Yes, it's very important to me and to my wife that they be removed from here, but not from the planet altogether."

"Don't worry about it a bit. There'll be some trauma for the little critters, or large rodents, I should say, but once we get them collected I've got the perfect place for them."

"Oh, do you know a zoo or something?"

"Zoo, oh no, that'd be worse than killing them in my book. By wonderful coincidence, I have a buddy that fishes up on the Taork River and he's mentioned a number of times how he wished there was a beaver dam nearby so he could have a better fishing hole. So here we are with a whole parcel of beavers with no place for 'em to be. It looks like I get to make a wish come true."

"That's outstanding. My wife will be very pleased to hear that, thank you."

"My pleasure, especially after you get my bill for this. It won't be cheap to round all these fellers up."

"That's ok. It's worth it to make sure they won't be destroyed."

"Well, it's a good thing you got a hold of me then, because most of the other exterminators 'round here would have just popped 'em off with a varmint rifle and sold what they could."

"Then I am glad indeed we got a hold of you. So

how long have you been doing this kind of thing?"

"Odd story that. My mother, not to speak ill of the dead, but my mother was really not the best housekeeper. There always seemed to be bugs of one sort or another around so I was never really bugged by 'em, if you know what I mean. One time there was this girl named Lucy. Boy, did I have a thing for her. Anyways, she got scared by a big bug once and I came to the rescue and felt like a hero. Even though she ended up marrying that loser Bill Krimley, the rush I got from protecting the fair maiden from the evil bug stuck with me. So after high school I went to a pest extermination class at the college and started my own business. I bet I learned more on my own before I even started the classes though; I was always fascinated by bugs. Yeah, I know insects; I just like saying 'bugs'. The official state certification license test was a joke, I even pointed out a few errors in the test. Nobody cared of course; you know how those things are."

Frank, with a small amount of amazement to himself, found himself asking, "So what's the oddest thing, besides this anyway, that you've had to catch or kill?"

A wry grim blossomed on the man's face. The gaunt man turned to look at the questioner and with an odd gleam in his eye, told his story.

"I got the call about four in the afternoon. Dark clouds were forming in the west above the Ciemne forest and I could feel *something* in the air. I was just finishing up spraying Mrs. Flavus' roses for aphids and a farmer over by the new commercial district between here and Conville called to say he had a rat problem and wanted me to come take a look. You know farmers are pretty darn good at dealing with rats, so I figured if he needed help it would be pretty interesting. I went over there and he showed me 'round to the back of one of his silos. Mind you, this wasn't one of those old wooden ones, but a nice, new one, made of aluminum and all. Down at the bottom of this shiny silo was big hole, all jagged and torn. I asked him if he couldn't just put out traps or didn't he have cats or dogs that could take care of this. He laughed and showed me the prints. They were monstrous. This rat had to be huge. I mean, I expected to see a whole bunch of little tracks based on the damage to the silo but there was only one set of tracks, and they were big. He looked at me with that pleading farmer look they do so well and asked if I would help him out. I did say 'wow', but also that I'd do what I could."

"I went back to my truck and picked out a few

choice tools and started following the spoor. Spoor, that's the trail an animal leaves, and if you're good, you can follow 'em wherever they lead. This trail headed towards the new business park they built out there a few years ago. I guess this rat had been going to the farmer's silo for a while 'cause the trail was pretty easy to see. It was just getting dark when I followed the trail to a large drainage pipe. Wouldn't ya know it; just as I was getting there I saw it. It was the biggest mother of a rat I ever saw, and mean-looking to boot. It saw me at the same time I saw him, or rather in this case, her. She bared her teeth all white and pointy, made a strange hiss and growl noise and scrambled all three and a half feet of its greasy, hairy body into the pipe."

"Honestly, it did take me a few seconds to decide on whether or not to go after it. I love a good hunt and this thing was surely a menace, but it was big and nasty, and like they say, the female of the species is usually the more dangerous. Then I thought about what would happen if this thing were to *breed*. I had images of giant rats taking over the planet and only the roaches being tough enough to survive. So I hiked up my pants turned on the flashlight I'd gotten from the truck and went in after it."

"As soon as I got in I flashed the light down the

tunnel of this drainage pipe. It was just big enough for me to walk down, all hunched-over like. I saw that big mamma just sitting up on its haunches looking at me. I'll be darned if it didn't have a *I-didn't-think-you'd-follow-me-in-but-let's-see-what-you've-got* look on its face. Those beady black eyes seemed to twinkle with red in the beam of my flashlight and then it spun around and headed down the tunnel. It was a long tunnel, a couple of hundred feet, easy. I figured I'd handle this the quick way and unstrapped the little .22 rifle I brought with me. Keeping the bugger in view with the flashlight in my left hand, you know steadying the rifle with that, I aimed right for the head. I thought for sure I had that sucker dead to rights and fired."

"I regretted it right away, the sound of that gun going off in the tunnel was like getting hit with two hammers right on each ear. After slinging the rifle back on my back, I put my hands up to my ears to see if I was bleedin' or not - it hurt that much. To make matters worse, instead of running away in a wild panic as I would have expected, that darn rat just stopped and looked at me as if it were curious, like it wasn't afraid at all. That scared me on one hand but made me even more sure that this Rattus rattus had to go the way of the Dodo Extincticus. A whole colony of these rats would be a horror. We all know the

Black Plague was carried around by rats, the filthy vermin playing horsy for the fleas that played horsy for the bacteria that killed half of Europe. So, with steely determination I walked down the long, dark tunnel toward my foe."

"When it saw me coming towards it, it shook its head a few times as if saying 'come on follow me', and I did. The foul beast skittered down the concrete shaft as if it were in no particular hurry. I must admit that this did get me a bit riled up. I'm used to vermin and other pests of man, but they're almost always runnin' from me and the chemicals I'm usually spraying around on them. This haughty beast was practically laughing at me. I lost sight of it only for a moment and then, there it was just sitting there, waiting for me. I thought about taking another shot at it, but my ears were still hurting from before, so I figured I'd bag this abomination with a net."

"I got about twenty feet away from it and figured I could sprint for a few and fling out my net. I paused for a moment to get the net ready then cut loose. Three steps into my sprint I realized I was at the edge of an abyss. It was a square room about ten feet across where all these other pipes joined into it. I stopped just on the edge, teetering over the brink and almost falling down.

I don't know how the rat got across it so fast and I swear it looked disappointed that I hadn't fallen down and broken my neck. The room looked like it went down about a hundred feet. Well, Ok, maybe in reality it was about thirty or so, but when you're hangin' out over your death it seems a whole lot more. The rat ran down the tunnel opposite the one we'd come from. I had to get over there and the only way I saw to get across was to go down and back up."

"There were these steel rings going up and down the side of the room like ladders, so I climbed down one side to the bottom. I half expected to find a pile of bones from all the others who had foolishly chased this monster down the tunnel, but there only a bunch of muck down there. I climbed up the other side and ran down the tunnel he way the rat had gone. I came to another room, about the same size, but the floor was even with the bottom of the tunnels. Some water was trickling out of some of the dozen or so other pipes opening into the room from above. I had to stop for a minute to catch my breath and to figure out which way to go."

"I heard it. I heard it's clacking, clittering claws on the hard concrete. They sounded more like the talons of some horrible were-beast out of an ancient fairy tale than claws of a modern-day rodent. I flashed my light down the tunnel that held the horrible sounds and caught another glimpse as it disappeared past a bend in the tunnel. I went a bit slower this time, checking my footing and being careful of the slippery goo that had collected in the bottom of the tunnels. There was another room with lots of tunnels branching off, so another choice."

"My ears were better now and I could hear it clearly. I didn't shine the light directly on the *Queen of All Rats*, as I was now calling it, so as to not scare it away, as if I could have. It had stopped in another room. This one only had small tunnels coming into it from the sides. I was afraid it would head down one of them and I wouldn't be able to follow it, so as soon as I was close enough, with that rotten, festering animal just sitting there waiting for me, I flung out my net. It was a perfect throw. It spun through the air and flattened out in a wonderful arc. I had the light down, so I was sure the net was invisible against the dark roof of the tunnel. That net landed just right. The rat spun around a few times squawking and chattering, but that only wrapped the net closer around it. I relaxed, figuring I had it, but as I got closer, I could see it biting on the net. It wasn't my biggest or strongest net, but I was sure it would hold."

"I was wrong. That thing chewed and clawed and ripped until it was free and it only took a few seconds. It looked at me and ran down the bigger tunnel. I drew my knife, I know, pretty stupid, but I grasped it hard in my hand and ran after it, screaming at the top of my lungs. Needless to say, I'd pretty much lost it by this point. Like an idiot, I tripped on the remains of my own net and went face down in the muck and algae in the middle of the tunnel. That stupid rat was scampering down the tunnel free as a bird. I got up and took off after it. As my flashlight swam back and forth across the tunnel while I ran, I noticed the end of the tunnel. It had a big grating over it, if I didn't get it before then, I never would. So I picked up speed and ran toward that hideous creature. Again I slipped on slime in the middle of the tunnel and fell not ten feet from the vile beastie. It looked at me with those beady eyes, those black balls of liquid tar, bulging from its pointy noggin and it chattered and turned to escape beyond the metal grating. I flung my knife at it as hard as I could in a final, desperate attempt to kill this evil creature. To my amazement, it flew true and nailed that rotten S.O.B. right in the middle. It let out a howling, screeching hiss and tumbled out past the grate."

"I was shocked that I actually hit it; the odds of

that were pretty low, I'm sure. I got up, went to the grate and wouldn't ya know it, the end of the tunnel was half way up a ravine that bottomed out to a stream. I found some blood near the opening, but I never found a body. The next day I went back to the lots and buildings above the tunnels, I even found the ravine and tunnel opening, but couldn't pick up a trail and never found my knife. I swear I would've mounted that sucker high on my wall if I could have. It would have been a beautiful sight. The farmer never had any more trouble with monster rats, so I assume I killed it, but boy I wish I knew for sure."

Mr. Wattle was still mesmerized by the man's tale, but managed to say: "Wow, that's quite a story. My wife's a big nature-lover, I wonder if even she would have tried to kill it."
"I don't know, but after she saw it, I bet she wouldn't have been the same. Outside of the giant rat, the worst thing I saw was a large colony of bats in a barn that hadn't been used for years."
"Wow, I bet that's a story too."
"Na, I just smoked 'em out and they moved on to someplace better. I just had an idea though, instead of trapping these poor beaver friends of yours, giving them all sorts traumatic memories, I've got a bunch of tranq darts I keep around for

mad dogs and such; people don't take kindly to you shooting their pets. Why don't I use them instead? I can cut the dose in half and take 'em out real quiet-like. I'm sure your wife will appreciate me not scaring them half to death by trappin' 'em up and such. It'll be real calm. I could even run 'em up to the Taork this afternoon if it doesn't take too long."

"That would be great, thanks."

"You go on back in and let her know I'll do my best to not hurt any of these little guys. I'll let you know when I'm done. Look out, here comes the fuzz."

Frank turned to see Chief Jardem walking up to the men. The chief explained he couldn't find any real evidence of how it was all done, or who might have done it. The only thing he did figure out was that ropes were used to slowly lower the trees and that must be why no one heard anything. Outside of that he saw no footprints or tire marks or anything else that might lead him to the culprit. He assumed the motive was Mrs. Wattle's proposal at the town meeting, but as almost everyone in town was there the suspect list was rather lengthy. Brewster and the chief started talking about different scenarios that would explain the situation and Frank walked back inside to his wife.

He explained the gentler solution to removing the beavers and she was pleased. He asked if she would like to go see the girls' softball game later that afternoon and was very happy when she said she would.

Brewster had no problem rounding up the beavers. They seemed very calm all the way up to the bend in the Taork River where he and his friend went fishing. He stayed for a while, making sure the beavers awoke from their induced rest without any problems. They slowly ambled off into the woods or towards the river. The sun had almost set by then, lighting up the sky with pinks, oranges, and greens. The birds stopped chirping, and so the frogs and crickets picked up the forest's euphonious chorus.

Chapter Five

Bottles

Susan Harrigan had nearly finished her morning run. She had a great routine. She'd start out with some stretching in the two-car garage. It was only half-used, as she only had the one car, so no matter the weather she would be protected from the elements while she prepared for her morning constitutional. After her warm-up and with the press of a button, the garage door would slide up and she would run off down the driveway and onto the road. Another button-press to the control in her jogging vest and the door would close behind her, keeping her house and possessions safe. She liked that feeling, in control, secure. Now she would run. She ran without music. Having those things in her ear felt like an invasion of her brain. The pounding of her footsteps set out the beat and rhythm of the time. After a loop around Saddle Road and the Bridle Hill development, she'd take off through the trees. The old fire trail was a perfect track. The old dirt and gravel road settled by many years of rain was just the right texture. It ran past her group of houses, curved up and over a modest hill then let out to route 7. She'd cross over with only a quick check of traffic, as there would be few cars out this early in the morning. Her path meandered about the older parts of town, one section filled with little more than shacks and others with beautiful old homes that seemed like models in a little girl's dream dollhouse town. A run down Main Street past Mary's Diner, half-filled with early risers let her know she was close to the end. A little further down she'd nod to store-keepers setting up for the day's business, then through the town's small park and back home for a breakfast of bananas and granola, a shower, then dress and off to work at the bank's main branch in the city.

As she neared her home, she pulled the remote from its pouch and clicked the button to open the garage door where she'd spend a few minutes cooling down and stretching some more before going inside the house proper. This time, as the door opened, something different happened. Instead of the welcoming empty expanse of the unused garage bay, something came out of the bottom of the door as it began to slide open. She almost expected this. In the span of a few short moments, she recalled the odd occurrences of the last weeks.

The first odd occurrence, she remembered, also happened with her returning from a morning run. An empty plastic water bottle was on the corner of her front step near the door. There was nothing special about it, just a generic-brand water bottle, empty and sitting upright; the clear plastic glinting in the morning sun. She thought little about it, brought it inside, and placed it among the other recyclables in her bright green container that sat in the corner of her kitchen. She carried on with her day as usual.

She recalled the next odd occurrence. Ms. Harrigan was in the grocery store. She would go to the larger store just outside of town, because they had a better selection of meats. Her high-protein diet made getting good meat a priority. She did her usual shopping, collecting fruits, vegetables, cereals and the leanest cuts of meat she could find. Although in her case, the cereals would only be of the crunchy granola variety. The rows of boxes with sugar infused, bleached, white flour only garnered a look of disdain. She was unloading her cart at the checkout stand and noticed a couple of items she didn't remember putting in.

She never bought commercial water bottles, or anything else that was incased in wasteful packaging that she could not easily recycle. So to see the two water bottles was rather odd. Even odder still because they were empty. They were not crunched or squished, maybe indicating they were trash left behind by the previous shopper. They were just two empty bottles, interestingly, of the same generic brand as the one found on her porch, she noticed. Thinking little of it again, she placed them in the bin for recyclables on her way out of the store.

Another odd occurrence happened a week after the shopping cart bottles. Every day after coming home from work, she would change into more comfortable clothes. She would then go to the kitchen to get a drink from the water cooler, a wonderful old-fashioned kind whose large glass bottle atop its steel pedestal would make a delightful blurb-gurgle sound with every large glass she filled. Then she'd go outside into the front yard and collect the day's mail. On this day, there was a little something extra in her bright green mailbox made from one-hundred percent post-consumer waste products, of which she was very proud. There were three empty water bottles. After the initial surprise of finding the unexpected items in her mailbox, she got a little upset. She assumed someone too lazy to throw the bottles away had just put them in her mailbox, another sign of the declining times. After thinking about it for a minute, however, she thought back to the bottle on her front step and then the bottles in her shopping basket and that triggered the memory of her proposal at the town meeting. Someone was teasing her. She thought for a few minutes about who it might be. Was it the guy a few houses down that had flirted with her the day she moved in? Maybe the two boys she always saw playing around town? Then she thought of something she hadn't before. Maybe it was someone intending to send a more serious message. But what was the message? Did they agree with her and wanted to point out all the wasted bottles? Did they disagree with the proposal and wanted to annoy her by making her responsible for all of *their* empty water bottles? She wasn't sure, but as they'd caused no real harm, she decided to put it out of her mind.

Standing on her driveway watching the final odd occurrence, she thought back to the odd occurrence that happened a few days after the mailbox incident. She would occasionally stop by the local donut shop for a cup of coffee on the way to work. Cheerfully handing the pimply, teenage boy her own coffee cup to fill with the steaming beverage. Proud of herself in resisting the urge to get a donut or danish, she went outside to resume her trip to the office. She got in, checked the mirrors then turned around to look. As she started to back up she heard a crisping, crackling crunch. Pressing hard on the brake, she looked around to see what she might have run over.

There was no one around. She thought maybe a friend of the coffee bar's employee had left their bike out near her car. She got out and looked around. There were four empty water bottles, each one now firmly planted beneath a tire. A wave of panic swept over her when she thought maybe there was something in the bottles that would damage her tires. She bent down for a closer look. No, they were only empty water bottles of the same generic brand she'd seen before. She pulled back up and went about collecting the unwelcome guests. No bin for recycling was nearby, so she put the bottles in her car for later disposal. She scanned the area, hoping to catch sight of the person responsible.

The streets were sparsely populated. She saw an elderly lady apparently walking her granddaughter to school and a jewelry store employee placing out an array of necklaces in the display window. Mr. Dips, pointed out to her earlier by one of the older residents as the town's drunk, was ambling down the far sidewalk. A few cars and trucks and the St. Albinus school bus were the only traffic on the roads. A young lady watering her flower pots on the third floor of the small apartment building up the block was about all else she could see. There were no signs of anything untoward going on. She sighed, more perplexed than angry and continued on to work.

She remembered there were no odd occurrences after that for a while. She went about her life as she saw fit. Working extra hours and doing everything she could to make sure she got that next promotion. Her morning runs and occasional weekend trips to the beach, wine tasting, or art exhibit kept her in a positive state of mind. She had made the connection between the bottles and the town meeting. She wondered why anyone would object to making the planet, or at least the town they lived in, a cleaner place. She hoped the offending prankster was only that, a prankster, and not some psycho that would continue to escalate the situation. Considering the fact that her proposal was now out of her hands, she had nothing more to do with it. She had only suggested it to the town council; it's not as if she were on the council deciding the fate of the proposal. Plenty of other towns had rules just like the one she proposed, it's not like her idea was all that radical.

As she stood at the bottom of the driveway and her heart pounded in her chest from her run, her mind raced back to the most unexpected of the

odd occurrences

Ms. Susan Harrigan, Vice President of Hamilton Federal Bank, got to the office early, as usual, checked her email for any overnight messages that would need her attention and looked over the progress of her ongoing projects. Her job screening loan requests was a good one, at least she thought so anyway. Many of her friends would tease her that she had one of the most boring jobs in the world. But to her, it was wonderful. Doing the research, checking the references, seeing plans people had for the future; it was a very good job. The feeling of power that came with the job was nice too. She realized it wasn't her money and she didn't have the final approval power - not yet anyway, but making sure all the I's were dotted and T's crossed gave her a sense of order in the universe. During her career at the bank she had gone from the person who did all the checking to the person who made sure other people did all the checking. Now she was one step away from the person that checked the people who check the people who checked. Proper forms, proper government approval, proper collateral, these were the things that made her world go 'round.

She checked the clock and was happy to see it

was almost ten. The courier came around ten. It was the courier who brought in new applications. The applications came in a particular box that would contain a new dream or an expanded empire. She enjoyed starting a new process. The files would need to be created, workflow processes would be initiated on the computer and the dance of numbers would begin.

Sure enough, this day she saw the courier, in his comfortable walking shoes, knee-length shorts, and her favorite: the clipboard. He would place the thin box on her desk, hand over the clipboard, and reach into his shirt pocket for the stub of a pencil. She often wondered why he always had a very small pencil for the receivers to sign with. How did he always have a short, yellow stub of a previously long number-two pencil? Did he spend his nights sharpening down nice new pencils into the squat, stubby things she was so familiar with? Did he have his children bring back pencils from school, those too short for even their little hands to do their sums, and give them to their father to use at work for some unfathomable reason? No matter what the reason, nor however the how, she enjoyed the ritual. She would take the stumpy writing implement and sign her special abbreviated signature to indicate reception. Now she was in charge of the package that might contain the start of the next major corporation, or the expansion of a current venture that would vault them to the top of their industry. A curt "thank you" and nod would conclude their exchange. She would watch him leave and wonder what other magic he would be delivering that day.

She centered the package on her desk. She ran her hands over the length just once, savoring the anticipation of the meaningful work that lay ahead. Grasping the thin, shiny, red plastic strip that ran alongside the short edge of the box, she pulled. A rather silly game it was, but when she opened these packages, she would make a prediction. If the box came open with a single swipe of the strip, then the project it contained would be a success, if not, then it was doomed to failure. She told herself that her assessment of the paperwork within would not be affected by her little game, and she believed it.

This one swiped open cleanly and easily. She lifted the flap and reached in for the envelopes that contained all the papers that would keep her and her team busy for weeks. She was already thinking of whom to assign the different jobs from this new request, when she felt something odd inside. There was more than just an envelope inside this package. Unable to identify the foreign object from touch, she stood up and dumped the contents of the rectangular box on her desk. There were five empty water bottles and a thick paper envelope. The bottles were crunched up and flattened, but that's what they were.

She felt trespassed on. Her work was her work, her career, a large part of her life. It was a thing separate from her home life. To intrude upon her here in the office was one step up from the other intrusions with empty plastic bottles. How did the prankster find out where she worked, or what delivery service they used, or that she would get a package today, or what package would go to her? All these questions bounced around in her head. It wasn't as if the prankster had sent a separate package straight to her. There on her desk was the standard loan request envelope. Could it be someone at one of the branch offices? No, it had come from a branch on the other side of the state, unlikely there'd be someone there who would have known about what went on in her local town meeting. Maybe there was more than one prankster. Maybe there was a whole network of people out there playing jokes on her. Now she was getting paranoid, she thought. The prankster must have intercepted the package and added the special odd items.

In a way she had to give a nod to the prankster, taking the effort to get all this done showed perseverance and determination if nothing else. Susan put the flattened bottles in the break room recycling bin and went back to the work she enjoyed. With a fresh stack of papers in front of her, she hoped this would be the last odd occurrence.

It wasn't. There was one other odd occurrence that she could remember. Before the one she was currently experiencing. She wasn't standing in her driveway, sweating and breathing heavily from her morning's exercise. She was out on a date. A first date in fact. Most of her dates were first dates. Her career took up most of her energy and she liked it that way. This date was another friend of a friend of a friend, as these things usually were. They were usually nice enough and she enjoyed going out occasionally. A nice dinner, movie, chatting at a fancy bar; it would be a nice time. It didn't really bother her that her friends thought she had to *have someone* in her life. Getting set up on blind dates every other month or so was not really all that bad. The evening was going well. He remembered his manners; she was in a good mood. They were having a nice time. After the movie, he suggested they go to a neat little pub he'd heard of. It was in Conville, not too far away. Susan Harrigan agreed that it sounded like a nice way to finish off the evening. Their drive would take them back through Boudton as the Cineplex was on the other side. They were chatting amicably, the dark outlines of trees sliding by in the car's windows unnoticed. The car's headlights would bring the blurring landscape into sharp relief as they passed by. She was only partway through her story of going to the zoo with her uncle when she was six; they had started to share safe and selected early childhood memories by that point, when he quickly slowed the car. In the road ahead, about halfway down a long, straight stretch of road, were six empty water bottles gleaming in the pale, blue beams of her date's headlights. Her evening's companion checked his mirrors in preparation for going around them when she asked him to pull over. As she got out to examine the now familiar, but still unwelcome guests, she started to feel creeped-out. This meant that someone knew her plans, or at least knew where she was and what she was doing. Maybe it was time to call the police. The unsettled feeling she got whenever she saw a water bottle anywhere now was getting uncomfortable. Wondering whether or when the next odd occurrence would happen, she picked up the bottles to dispose of properly at a later time.

The rest of the evening was uneventful. She managed to not explain to her date the other events with empty water bottles, and was grateful for it. Telling the story would make her seem too much like a victim. There were a few more childhood revelries to exchange and as the evening waxed late, her date started slipping into sports metaphors concerning the office politics that seemed to swarm about him daily. It was getting late, so she asked him to take her home. She said goodnight in the driveway with him still in the car and let herself into the garage with the opener as she preferred it to the front door. It had been a picture of a pleasant evening, with only a mild smudging from another bottle incident.

And now this, indeed the oddest of the odd occurrences. Her leg muscles twitched from the stress of the recent workout. Her brain raced, and was losing, to try and comprehend what it was she saw. As the garage door, usually a secure guardian of her comfortable home now turned into a deliverer of oddness as it separated from the ground and released a horde of empty water bottles. They spilled out onto the driveway, tumbling and bouncing over each other in a mad dash down her driveway. The wider the door opened, the more bottles poured forth. Down they came, cascading across the clean, white concrete. When the first of the bottles set free had just reached her feet and were bouncing off of her worn, but still very comfortable cross-trainers, the door reached the peak of its climb and the bottles came out at a full torrent.

She couldn't see her feet or ankles anymore, but still she stood there, fixed on the scene. Mouth agape, mind spinning with the ruminations of the past few months, she stood there, trying to absorb it all. Even with all that had happened and what it might mean, or the danger that could easily have been caused instead of harmless practical jokes, she thought it was beautiful. The flow of the crystal-clear bottles and the way they jumped and bounced and frolicked with each other as they raced down the driveway and spread out on to the street in front of her house struck her as nothing but stunning. All other sounds had ceased, only the crackling, crinkling sound of the bottles against one another seemed to exist. Thoughts of cleaning them up weren't in her head yet.

It was such a strange sight, strangely lovely and definitely the oddest thing she had ever seen. Susan Harrigan then began to laugh. It was a hearty laugh. It was deep and true because it came from far inside herself. She had not laughed like this in a long time. Certainly she had given the respectful chortle to the boss's latest joke or family anecdote. She had snickered with her friends as they made fun of some poser at a wine festival. There were even a few titters when an off-color joke was made concerning one of her friend's husbands. But this was a true laugh, the contagious kind, the honest sound of deep amusement. This was not a guffaw like a hillbilly after too much moonshine nor was this the cachinnation that the trouble-makers in the back of her high school English class would be accused of by old Mr. Harrison. Thus she stood there laughing, enjoying the hilarity of it all. Even though the joke was on her, she could not escape the humor in the situation.

Another sound then reached her ears. It too was a laugh, but it wasn't hers. It was much lower, a man's laugh. She turned to see the town's chief of police standing a few yards away. Tears were streaming down his cheeks and he was laughing as hard as seemed possible. The rotund belly of the town's old cop jiggled back and forth and shook with the intensity of the activity. He noticed her looking at him and with a very contrite look on his face, held up his hand as if to say "Sorry, I am so sorry, I don't mean to laugh, but you have to admit…" The smile on his face was genuine and the sound of his laughing made her laugh that much harder. They stood that way for minutes, with empty water bottles piling up around them and laughing like they didn't care.

When they finally got hold of themselves, after gasping for breath, only to have the fit return multiple times, they calmed down and the smiling policeman with a now rubicund face said,

"You're Ms. Harrigan Yes? I'm so sorry to laugh. I really don't mean to. But when I saw all those bottles come rushing out of your garage and then you started laughing, well I just couldn't help myself. "
"No chief, it's quite alright, I completely understand. If you *weren't* laughing I'd probably think there was something wrong with you. Yes, Susan though, if you please. What are you doing here, you didn't have anything...?"
"Oh, no. I was just 'in the neighborhood' as they say. There have been a few incidents in the area since the town meeting surrounding the people who made proposals. So officer Vlad and I have been making a few extra patrols in the area. It looks like I was just a bit too late. I am assuming you didn't put those bottles there, is that correct?"
"Correct, they are not my bottles."

"How long have you been out of the house, it looks like you were out for a walk or something?"

"Yes, I just finished my regular morning jog. It usually takes about forty-five minutes."

"Only that long, huh? Hmm. Well, it seems our bottle deliverer is quick on his feet. I can't imagine how anyone could get that much into a garage so quickly. I don't suppose you saw any large trucks on your morning jog, did you?"

"No, I'm afraid I didn't. I wasn't going to say anything before this anyway, but I have had a few odd occurrences with other empty, plastic water bottles. There was one left on my front porch and in my shopping cart and at work even and on the road a little bit ago, it's been going on for a few months now - like you said, since the town meeting. I made a proposal to start charging a deposit on all bottles, so that people would be motivated to recycle, it's one of my pet peeves, I'm afraid."

"Well, I am sorry to hear that you've been hassled of late. So far we haven't had any luck in figuring out who's been doing these things, and thank goodness no one's been hurt or anything. Just some minor property damage so far. I don't want you to think we take trespassing lightly around here; what with me laughing like a hyena and all. We'll do some investigating and try our best to get to the bottom of this. If you have any

further incidents, or occurrences, please contact myself or Officer Voet right away."
Yes, I will thank you"
"Are you all right now; would you like me to check the house before you go in?"
"No, I'm sure I'll be fine. They've only been pranks, like you say; I'll call if I need anything."
"Very well then, I'll be outside here for a while making my report and looking to see if there's any evidence of who might have done this. Tell me, was the garage locked?"
"Yes, you need the remote to open or close it and the rest of the house should have been locked up as well, I usually don't leave things open."
"Does anyone else have a spare key or extra opener?"
"No, I live alone and all my family is back in the city, so as far as I know, no one else has a key."
"Thank you for the information, you take care now. And again, I am sorry for laughing at your misfortune; it's not very professional and all that."
"No problem, chief, don't worry about it. Though the problem I do have now is how to clean all these up. I don't think all these bottles will fit in my kitchen recycling bin."
"No, I don't suppose they would. I have seen a recycling company truck around here before, I think when Mr. Kepen passed away and his niece

found a whole lifetime's worth of newspapers
stacked in piles in every room in the house. They
called a place from Conville, I'll see if I can find
the name of the company for you. In the
meantime, I'll get the road cleared, so we're not
causing a traffic hazard. I think the fire house
has a bunch of brooms, they'll probably enjoy a
job like this, and they're usually pretty bored.
Well, the old timers anyway, who don't have a
day job and end up sitting around the station all
day checking equipment or playing checkers or
some such."
"Thanks chief, that would be great."

Officer Voet pulled up just as Susan Harrigan
disappeared inside the front door. He and the
chief spent a number of minutes looking around
for any clues. There didn't seem to be any
evidence of tampering at any of the doors. The
most obvious way in, concluded Officer Voet,
was the automatic garage door. As the opener
was a simple radio transmitter, it wouldn't be
much of a stretch to imagine someone making a
device that cycled through all the frequencies
until it found the right one. Or even easier than
that, the chief suggested, would be to set up
some sort of recorder that would listen when the
real opener was used and then it wouldn't be
much trouble setting a transmitter to emit the

same signal. They looked around a bit more, but as the device could have been placed almost anywhere and most likely had been removed from wherever it might have been, they didn't expect to find it. They went about a less interesting job, but one more likely to bring results, and interviewed the neighbors, asking if they'd seen an unusual truck in the area, or anything else suspicious.

They met back up in front of Ms. Harrigan's house neither one of them having any luck finding a witness. The chief asked Officer Vlad if he would mind calling up Kepen's niece and then letting Ms. Harrigan know who she used to empty out her uncle's house. The chief said he was going to the fire house to see if he couldn't get someone to come over and get the road cleared. Officer Voet was to stay at the house to handle any traffic problems until the volunteers arrived.

The volunteer firefighters were only too happy to help clean up. Sitting around in the firehouse waiting for a call that only rarely came, they were glad to get out and do something. The shiny red truck pulled up and parked down the street a ways. Seven people showed up, four men and three women. The women were technically from the fire brigade auxiliary, as all the women chose to be. They did all the same jobs as the men, but enjoyed their own special club and meetings without the men whenever they wanted. The Boudton Volunteer Fire department had the road cleaned up in under an hour. They even cleaned up Ms. Harrigan's driveway and emptied the garage of the remaining bottles.

They were heaped up in a rather impressive pile on the side yard, ready for the recycling company to come by and pick them up. Ms. Harrigan came out and offered the volunteers coffee before she had to head out for work. They declined the offer, as the firehouse coffee was a particular source of pride with the members. Their sometimes vicious insults of anyone else's coffee were a constant source of amusement to them. The volunteers found out that the recycling company would not be charging Ms. Harrigan anything to come pick up the bottles, considering the number of bottles, they would be making quite a bit for selling them to the center that then sold them back to various bottling companies and other recycled product companies. Susan was very pleased to know that they wouldn't just end up in a landfill someplace.

Deputy Fire Chief Alan Price made sure everything was squared away before he headed back to the station. They all had a good laugh at the mountain of bottles; strange things were indeed afoot in their usually quiet, little town. Back at the station, they stowed their gear, cleaned up the truck, which was always kept bright and shiny, and went about the other tasks of the day.

Later that afternoon, Alan Price went to Mary's Diner for a meal of minestrone soup and a grilled-cheese sandwich. While he sat and ate, he watched the town out the window that faced Main Street and thought about what a nice place it was. For fifty-three years this place had been his home and he couldn't imagine any other place being so right. From the looks of the buildings to the smell of the trees, this place was home. But then, he thought, any place you spend that many years in would be home as well. A bustling metropolis, a hectic port town, or an isolated farming hamlet; all these places would be home for those who lived there.

Then his mind drifted off to people who maybe were not home. His thoughts passed over an anxious youth brought up in a small, rural hamlet who couldn't stand the small-town yokels, with their small thoughts and small words, even the people he'd been friends with his whole life. Then Mr. Price's thoughts flittered

over to a harried businessman who would rather
be tending sheep in a high alpine pasture than
going to the endless, mindless meetings he was
subjected to on a daily basis. Next he thought of
a poor fisherman's son, in Indonesia maybe, who
often thought of living in Paris with the beautiful
people, going to fancy parties and luxurious
restaurants and never again setting foot on
another boat in his life. Alan Price considered
himself lucky, as he was where he wanted to be.
He only wished for another bowl of Mary's soup;
as his had been emptied completely.

Chapter Six

Smoke

Mr. Nicholas Jean sat in his den. By his wife it was also called; man-cave, pit, hole in the basement, or, *that pig-sty you refer to as a den.* He didn't mind. The rest of the house had to remain clean. Here he could have things as he wished, and he wished them messy. Stacks of magazines, half he'd never read, lined the floor. Shelves groaning with a lifetime of memories slouched below the small half-window that could barely let any light in between the clutter on the sill. An array of recognition plaques peppered one wall, most of them tilted at odd angles. There were Employee of the Month plaques with brass bars on wooden bases, Highest Standards in Record-keeping certificates in cheap plastic frames, and high-game awards with crossed bowling pins, among many others. The desk was a mess of bills, instruction manuals for household appliances, and newspapers from the last few weeks. His feet were also on the desk. Stretched out behind the threadbare, knit slippers was Mr. Jean relaxing in his chair. It was a most comfortable chair. An old wood and leather job with clanky coasters that let him slide across the linoleum floor.

He was doing nothing, nothing but relaxing and eyeing up the plaques on the wall. The biggest was from his retirement dinner. Forty years he worked in that warehouse, most of it as the head man. He had thought of it as his kingdom. No one knew more about where things were or how the system operated. Parts and supplies, equipment and shelving systems had become such a part of his life that he never knew for sure he could retire until he actually did it. That was two years ago. At times he was sorry he waited so long. The freedom to do what he wanted, and when, was very intoxicating. At least here in his den he could eschew all the organization he was subjected to for those forty years. On *his* shelves things didn't have to be labeled. On *his* shelves he could put anything he wanted anywhere he wanted. No corporate mandates or government regulations had to be followed in this place. There would be no inspections by brainless busybodies; this was truly *his* kingdom. This was truly *his* time.

He feared being retired would kill him, dead from boredom. Instead it made him more alive. His years of working and saving had really paid off for his current relaxation. He had finally moved out to the country. He was no longer tied to being in close proximity to the warehouse. He and his wife had found these great new homes, out off the beaten path, but not too far away that he couldn't visit his son back in the city whenever he wanted. He could mow the lawn during the week, in the middle of the day, instead of spending precious weekend time. He could sleep late, if he chose. He could wear nice clothes during the week instead of having to don the azure shirt and work trousers as per company policy, or he could wear the rattiest, threadbare shorts he had, anytime he wanted. Movies and dinners out were no longer confined to Friday nights as they had been for the last forty years. He could take his wife out to eat, without making reservations on a Tuesday, and the movie theater would not be crowded with hordes of boisterous teenagers acting up for their friends or the chattering girls. He was even looking forward to voting this year, during the day, ten-thirty perhaps, when no one else would be waiting in line. "Forget the so-so old days - these would be the good new days," he found himself saying more than once.

He liked the town of Boudton. It was small enough where everyone seemed friendly and big enough where he could still enjoy most of the conveniences he had enjoyed when he lived back in the city. He had spent most of the first few months living here trying to find all the neat places and comfortable spots that he would like to visit often. He liked The Empty Pump, its casual attitude and friendly bartender would make a nice place to go when he wanted to get out of the house. On his first trip to the local watering hole he started to sit on what he thought would be the best bar stool, but was kindly warned off by the bartender that *that* one belonged to Mr. Dips, one of his more consistent customers, and would he mind sitting anywhere else he chose. Mr. Jean found that quaint and nice, that the regulars' spots would be protected by the owner.

He went to the bar occasionally after that and met a few of the other regulars, none as regular as Mr. Dips, he found out. They were all normal guys, decent people who had their drinks, talked with friends and just enjoyed the ambiance. The atmosphere was nice, apart from the big guy that came in once and lit up a monster stogie. Nicholas was glad he sat near the end of the bar and most of the smoke was taken up by the ventilator, else he was sure the bar would have emptied out. He was on friendly talking terms with a few of the patrons, and had considered whether or not to ask the older men in the corner if he could sit in on a few hands of their weekly poker game. He never had though; he figured he'd be better off going home and not smelling overly of beer and cigars.

He tried Mary's Diner as a place to get an easy meal out, but the one time he went there it was a bit crowded and the only seats left were in the smoking section. The waitress was nice enough and competent, but the smoke wafting around him from the other diners was just too much. He eventually found a nice *greasy spoon,* as he called it, a few miles out of town. It was a shame; he thought the diner in town would have been much more convenient.

One part of Mr. Jean's schedule that hadn't changed was his Saturday afternoon cook-out. It would be a choice piece of meat, carefully chosen and purchased the day before. It would be carried home gently; he would have no bruises on this broad slab of happiness. Those savage animals who beat and pound their steaks with pointed mallets to tenderize them were fools in the mind of Mr. Jean. A marinate of secret spices and oils would spend the night cradling and insinuating itself into the thick juicy flesh, transmuting the hunk of meat into ambrosia.

He admired the glistening cut as he pulled it from the refrigerator. The fork pierced the dark pink flesh and carried it from the negative-pressure marinating dish to the outdoor platter. This large wooden platter with a deeply engraved carving of a bull's head served as a litter for the meal's honored main course. The aroma of fresh meat and spices had already started his mouth to watering. Carefully carrying the day's feast out onto the back patio, he lovingly placed the loin cut next to the grill.

His grill was custom-made, one of the first things he did after moving in was to have the grill built to his specifications. The shining stainless steel shell set in a stone embrace shone in the afternoon sun. The removable drip tray, side burners and thermometer all awaited his command. The button for the automatic starter stood ready beneath his poised finger. When he lifted the lid to watch the blue flame dance as the grill *foomed* to life, he was very much surprised.

Instead of the familiar grate upon which he would place his inchoate meal there was instead a large mound of cigarette butts. There were all sorts of cigarettes in the pile filling the inside of the grill. Ones with tan filter ends, ones with white ends, there were even cigarillos with their all brown wrappings. A few cigar butts populated the mass as well, looking like fat freckles or moles amid the lighter shades. He immediately looked around, half-expecting to see a bunch of his old friends from the warehouse laughing at their good-natured, practical joke. There was no one around. A few birds flew above the trees beneath high, thin clouds. His wife, he knew, was in her sitting room reading a magazine and patiently waiting for him to finish with his weekly ceremony of *caveman cuisine.* When he figured out it wasn't a joke he got a bit upset. This was *his* Saturday afternoon, his favorite time of the week, when he cooked his own food as he wished and ate it outside, as he wished. *Al fresco,* as his old friend Nathan would always remind him, no matter how many times he had before. "This is vandalism", he said to himself, "I shouldn't have to take this".

He started to go and phone the police, but thought instead he'd wait and go personally on Monday and talk with the chief. He'd met Chief Jardem a week or so before in the Empty Pump. They'd had a nice conversation and Nicholas had even bought the chief a beer, his way of thanking him for helping secure the safety of the town. Since he figured he was on speaking terms with the chief of police, maybe he'd get better answers in person. He had also heard while around town and in the Pump that a sort of crime-wave had been taking place in this usually placid little town. Maybe this was part of the same spree. His proposal to ban smoking in the town was tickling the back of his mind.

Mrs. Jean was a bit surprised to find out the evening's steak was broiled in her oven instead of on his grill as usual. The sour look on his face at dinner convinced her not to ask why.

Monday morning at ten o'clock, Mr. Nicholas Jean presented himself at the police station. He found Officer Voet sitting at the front desk and asked if he could have a word with the chief. After a short trip to the back room the young officer informed him that the chief would be happy to see him now. Mr. Jean was led into a small office, dimly lit through the half-closed blinds on the window. A few plaques like his own were scattered around the walls. A large picture of the town hall on its dedication day with the fading signatures of the attendees hung on the wall behind the desk. A cheerful-looking Chief Jardem stood to shake hands.

"Well, good morning Nick, nice to see you again. It's a bit early for a drink isn't it? Or are you here to have me pay for that beer by fixing a parking ticket?" A wide grim warmed his face.
"Not at all, that drink was an honest gift to thank

you for putting yourself on the line for all of us. I would never use that as a lever to push a favor. Rather, I've come to see you about a more serious matter. I've heard talk around town of some strange events that seem to be related to suggestions raised at the last town meeting. I may have another one."

"Well, I see, another one, eh? Why don't you tell me about it?" He motioned to a chair and sat down himself.

"I had a trespasser sometime this week. On Saturday afternoons I cook up steaks for the wife and I, it's one of my favorite routines, only this time when I went to cook my expensive steaks, I found that someone had filled my grill with cigarette butts. I was going to call you right then and there, but thought it would be better to come in person. I haven't yet cleaned up the grill in case you need to do some sort of forensic investigation, but I wanted to get from you first-hand what might be going on."

"Well, that sounds about right. That's the kind of thing that has been going on around here of late. You do realize that a *suggestion*, as you call it, made in front of the town council, is proposing a law and a law means me and my pistol? Laws are serious things, and many folks don't take kindly to being told they *have* to do something or *can't* do something. But, deciding what is or isn't a law is not my job. It *is* my job to enforce the law, however, and there already are laws about trespassing and littering, so let's go out and see what happened."

"Thank you chief. I've saved my whole life to be able to retire and live in peace; I shouldn't be treated like this."

"Well, I'm not treating you like that, and I'll do my best to find out who is. I hope your meal wasn't ruined, did you find some other way to enjoy your steak?"

"Actually I did. Broiled it in the wife's oven and it turned out pretty good. Maybe on the cold, winter afternoons that will be coming up before we know it, I'll do some Saturday cooking indoors. As long as I can convince *Mrs.* Jean that I will actually clean up after myself."

"Well, that's a good attitude; now let's go see if we can find anything at the scene of your crime."

As with the other incidents, there were no obvious clues as to who may have done it. The butts could have come from anywhere. Of all the different brands that could be identified, there were no special, odd, or weird ones. There wasn't even a brand that stood out due to their number. It was clear that they were carefully chosen so as to give no indication of where they might have come from. The chief suspected they may have come from the Empty Pump, but if that were the case then he would have seen an abnormally large amount of the brand Nate and Turner smoked, as they were famous for the amount of cigarettes they were always seen puffing on. Chief Jardem warned Mr. Jean to look out for any further incidents, as sometimes there was more than one.

The chief went back to the station to file the reports and Nicholas Jean cleaned out his grill thinking about what to cook next Saturday. He wondered if he could get some lamb at the local store, it had been a while since he grilled up a nice lamb roast and it would give him a good chance to use his new rotisserie attachment.

A few weeks later, near Mr. Jean's front walk, dew glistened in the morning sun. The thick green leaves lining the sidewalk of the Jeans' front yard held up the drops as if making an offering to the returning rays of light pouring in from the east. Ants near the stalks began their single-file march across the weed-free beds of the worshipping plants. An earthworm, gardener to the world, squiggled to the surface and wrung about for a few moments before plunging back down into the depths to burrow and bore out of sight of any hungry bird. A silent cricket hopped and bounded from the grass on the other side of the walk to rest beneath the broad leaves of the healthy flora. A chipmunk raced along under the cover, its tail a flashing pennant among the stalks. It would pause briefly to look around and then continue its hectic pace along the edge of the yard. All seemed fine and right to the faunae. The woodland creatures sensed nothing amiss. But to the human animals standing on the front porch, with peculiar looks on their faces, something was indeed amiss. Instead of the petunias, mums, and marigolds, they had planted only a few short months ago, there were instead, the dark-green and hairy leaves of tobacco plants lined along their front walk. Mr. and Mrs. Jean were standing there, her with curlers in her hair, and he with a phone to his ear, trying to explain to the chief of Boudton's police department what they were looking at. It was trespassing and theft, to be sure, and Chief Jardem would be right on his way out.

No clues again, though it didn't take long to find out what had happened to his plants. The Boudton Garden Club called around one o'clock in the afternoon to report a strange incident in the park. The town park was where they tended the rose bushes and other assorted plants ringing the large grassy area hemmed in with hedges just across from the new housing development of Bridle Hill. There were extra plants in the park now, and none of the garden club knew where they had come from. They were surprised to hear that the chief knew exactly what kind of plants had been added to the town's display. They weren't the kind of plants the garden club would have chosen, but they looked rather nice nonetheless. The chief gave Mrs. Poliverde, the club leader, a brief explanation and asked if they would take care of the plants until Mr. Jean came for them or request that they stay there.

The chief called up Nicholas to let him know they'd found his plants. He did have to explain that the town would not pay to have them moved back and replanted, but suggested he call the garden club and maybe they would be willing to help him if he didn't want to do it himself.

On a Thursday morning, a few weeks later, Deputy Fire Chief Alan Price heard the alarm. He was in the second-floor kitchen of the fire house, looking over the week's maintenance schedule and eating a poppy-seed bagel smeared with strawberry cream cheese and drinking his second cup of exquisite firehouse coffee. He ran downstairs to the alarm panel and saw it was an automated alarm. It was from one of the new homes out at Bridle Hill. The new houses all had fancy fire and burglar alarm systems, one of their many selling points. While he knew a lot of these automated systems gave out false-positive alarms, he still treated it with the same urgency he would as if his most trusted friend had called and told him first-hand. There were only three other fire brigade volunteers on-duty right now, but he knew the others that lived or worked close-by would be there in a matter of minutes. He and the others at the station went about donning their gear and getting the truck ready to pull out. While they were starting the truck, removing wheel-chocks and otherwise prepping the vehicles for the trip, five other volunteer firemen and firewomen had arrived and were busy getting ready. The last of them were prepared and hopped on the truck as it pulled out. With DFC Price at the wheel, they traveled as safely, but as quickly, as they could the short two and a half miles across town to the address. The riders waved to people they knew as the sirens echoed between the building and set off a litany of barking dogs. They sped toward the scene of emergency like a loud, red carnival float. They could see the smoke before they were even past the park. A thick, gray-green haze was washing across the park from the gap in the trees made by Saddle Road and the opening to Bridle Hill.

With air brakes hissing and the siren dying off, the bright red truck pulled up to a stop mid-way between the nearest fire hydrant and the house.

While DFC Price jogged towards the house to begin the assessment of how to attack the fire, a hectic ballet of purposeful movement played out behind him. They practiced drilling for such an occasion every weekend, but when a real call came in, it was different. There were far fewer jokes and smiles. A real call wasn't an enjoyable afternoon with friends and family doing important work, and also looking forward to the cook out or pot-luck dinner waiting for them when they finished. This was real. Real lives and real property were at stake and each volunteer worked as if it were their home on the line, as if it were their lifetime of belongings being devoured by the dangerous servant of fire.

Alan Price found two people standing out on the lawn in front of the house. He was grateful to hear the answer of "No one", when he asked if there was anyone still inside. The woman looked distraught and the man looked concerned. The man also looked helpless as he stared at the house, his home, spewing smoke from every orifice.

DFC Price started formulating his plan on how best to extinguish the fire that was surely gutting the house as he stood there looking. However, the longer he looked the odder he knew something was. There was plenty of smoke all right, but where he expected to see tongues of flame licking up the side of the house through the open windows, he only saw more smoke. The entry team had made it up to him and they stood ready with axes and sledges, ready to fight their way to the source of the fire, or to rescue any one left inside. He told them no rescuing was needed only the source of the fire to find. With their air tanks strapped to their backs and masks securely in place they strode towards the base of the gray tower of smoke before them. The front door stood open, only partially revealed between billows of dark, gray fumes. He made sure to ask the owner if there were any large stores of dangerous chemicals inside and being assured by the man there were none, he slowly moved into the interior of the house.

The team slowly stalked through the entranceway, carefully on the lookout for dangers hidden in the smoke. They turned right into the living room with its couch and chairs facing a coffee table filled with picture books. The light breeze picked up a bit and the room had cleared slightly. DFC Price noticed the smoke was pouring out from the heating vents. He called out, "Let's find the furnace." They turned in unison and headed back to the front hall. One of the other volunteers located a door that looked like it should lead to the basement,

and after checking for excessive heat behind it,
slowly pulled it open. When he saw the young
woman check the door for heat, it struck DFC
Price that the house was cooler than it should
have been. In the other, only a few, but in the
other house fires he had been in there was an
oppressive amount of heat everywhere. Pushing
the thought aside for the moment, he took the
lead down the stairs. The bare wooden steps
creaked beneath the weight of the town
firefighters in all their gear. The smoke was
thicker in the basement, the powerful halogen
flashlights barely showing four feet in front of
them. In a few moments, they found the furnace
and it was indeed belching smoke from every
crack and seam. Upon closer inspection he
noticed the smoke was coming down the flu.
Where smoke should have been going up the
exhaust pipe there was a torrent of smoke
coming down. Another idea hit him now. He
radioed out to the hose team standing ready on
the front lawn and asked if anyone could see the
furnace chimney outlet and was there any smoke
coming out from it. The response he got was
that neither the fireplace chimney nor the
furnace chimney had much in the way of smoke
coming out. "We need to find the attic." was the
next muffled but still clear order from the
deputy fire chief.

The team moved back out of the basement then up the main steps to the second story. The large boots of the fire team left deep, treaded footprints in the soft carpeting. Once on the second floor, they could see the hatch to the attic about halfway down the hallway. Again feeling for heat before opening it and a slow tentative pull on the string hanging below it, the door swung down. There was hardly any smoke coming in from the attic and the rest of the team exchanged curious glances. With the thin attic steps groaning under the weight of DFC Alan Price, he ascended into the attic.

They went one at a time, not trusting the flimsy stairs which were barely more than a ladder. The DFC could see easily up here with light flowing in from the vents at each end of the steeply slanted room. The first thing he noticed was a light bulb missing from its socket. In its place there was an orange extension cable plugged in where the bulb belonged. He followed the cord to its home and found a machine, about the size of a small generator with a large tube coming from it and going in to an access panel in the side of what must have been the furnace chimney. A large jug was sitting on top of the machine with a tube running from it to a small tank on the side of the device. Deputy Fire Chief Alan Price pulled off his glove, reached out for a

switch on the side of the machine and flicked it
down into the off position. The machine's hum
lowered in volume and pitch and wound down to
a halt. The only sound now was that of their
breathing apparatus. The five sets of clicking
and hissing mechanisms mingled with faint calls
of birds outside the attic vents.

A quick radio call was made outside to let the
hose team know they wouldn't be needed and to
start packing the equipment back up. The
inspection team disconnected the machine from
both power and the vent. And not unlike the
ants in Mr. Jean's flowerbed, the firefighters filed
out from the attic, making a brief visual
inspection of the rest of the house, and ended
up out front again. Explaining what they found
to the homeowners only took a few minutes. The
police chief had arrived by then and he seemed
to know Mr. Jean and was much better at
handling public relations. The deputy fire chief
was much more at home cleaning a pump or
stacking a hose than he was at dealing with
someone else's misfortune. He was able to report
that the movie magic smoke machine probably
did very little actual damage. It wasn't like the
smoke from a real fire that would often do more
damage than the flames. At least from what he
had observed, a small fire that he and his
volunteers could put out quickly was nothing

compared to the smoke that would affect the entire house, and everything in it, even if the fire was just a small one in the basement. Thankfully, all he had to do was deliver his report and let the chief handle whatever fall-out there may be. The Boudton volunteer fire company could get back to their work of stowing the gear and getting ready for the next emergency. A few in the company were disappointed, he could tell from their faces. Not really upset that someone's house had not been destroyed, but the excitement of a real fire to put out was one reason many of the volunteers volunteered. For some, the allure of adventure was what drew them to hours of training and practice. They went about their work putting things away, uncoupling hoses and loading the truck for the return trip to the station where there would be hours more work cleaning and prepping. They would work knowing the real value of their service was to save lives and property, but they had missed the excitement of a real emergency.

Mr. Jean and his wife went back into their home after the all-clear was given. While walking through the house with the chief and ending up inspecting the strange machine in the attic there had been little talk. A few nicks and scratches around the soffit explained how the interloper had gotten the machine into the house. No living space was violated directly by the miscreant but the feeling of violation could not be avoided. Mrs. Jean was particularly affected. It would take a few weeks of Nicholas' assurance and double-checking of the doors and windows until she would feel safe again.

Johnny and Bobby made another trip out to Bridle Hill that day after school. Few traces remained of the incident, mainly just a pool of water near the recently flushed hydrant. Heavy boot prints on the front grass and fans in a number of windows was all that remained. They looked at each other, disappointed, and decided to head over to Mac's Run and play for a while in the stream. Maybe the dam they built last week would still be there. Hopefully some small guppies would be swimming around in the backed-up water. That would make for a few hours of good playtime until they would have to go back home. When they would have to eat whatever vegetables their mothers would force upon them at dinner, do whatever homework their teachers would load them up with, then they could watch a little bit of TV before they had to go to bed. Then they would dream of rescuing the surely-doomed residents of a big house being consumed by an even bigger fire that would make them heroes.

CHAPTER SEVEN

MARY'S DINER

On Main Street, right in the middle of town, was Mary's diner. The first Mary was Mary Winchester, an older woman, who arrived from parts unknown, with a teenaged daughter. She caused some grumbling when she bought what used to be Oscar's Clothing Store; empty since the previous owners had died a year and a half before. The grumbling didn't last very long. Though some missed the local clothing store, very few would have traded back after they had tasted her cooking. Her beef stew alone made many memories of a mother's stew vanish in a wisp of delicious steam. She was a very pleasant woman and her daughter was always cheery and helpful to the customers when she waited on them. No one ever found out the original Mary's story, even her daughter didn't seem to know very much, or at least, never talked about it. Her name was Mary as well. When her mother died, many years and many full bellies later, the only thing that wasn't left to her daughter was the recipe for that wonderful beef stew. Not that there was anything wrong with the second Mary's stew, but those who remembered the original, never seemed to forget it.

The second Mary married Tom Srung, the son of the proprietor of the jewelry store next door to the diner. After a few years they had a Mary of their own. This was the Mary who cooked for, and cheered up, the town now.

The diner was a focal point of sorts for the town. It was a place where many of the town's residents would gather to enjoy reasonably good food and casual conversation. The big front windows fed a view of Main Street into the whole interior. In the winter months, the windows would fog up with steam from beef stew, greasy burgers, freshly baked bread, or whatever the soup of the day was.

Each patron of the venerable diner seemed to have their own unique memory of the place.

For Mrs. Parker it was the time she found a pair of the second Mary's reading glasses in her bowl of turkey barley soup. With nothing more than a "So *that's* where they went." and "Let me get you a fresh bowl." Mary went merrily about with the rest of her work. Never being able to find out the story behind the enigmatic first Mary, Mrs. Parker ate at the diner more often than one would have thought. Hoping to hear or cajole a word or two about Mary's mother, Mrs. Parker would ask about ingredients or the story behind a certain dish, but to no avail, the secrets of the first Mary were veiled behind a failing memory or a clever deflection. Although with so many of the other town's residents stopping by for food and drink, Mrs. Parker did manage to glean quite a bit of information about everyone else in the town.

For Chief Jardem it was his daughter's wedding reception that provided him with a singularly wonderful memory. She was told by her parents she could have the reception anywhere. Even in the fancy hotel in the city if she wished. They had saved for this day and wanted it to be special. However, for the daughter, having it at Mary's would be the most special it could be. And it was, from Mary's tears of joy for the way the young woman felt about her diner to the way the place had been decorated like never before. Quite a few people remembered that event. Seeing their normally stoic police chief weep in public even harder than the new bride caused many another tear to roll down a cheek in Mary's Diner on that day.

For Bobby the special memory came on his twelfth birthday, in the form of a special bike. It was the exact one he had wanted. Bobby's mother, not being much of a cook, would have

her children's birthday dinner at Mary's diner.
The birthday boy or girl could have anything on
the menu and Mary would cook one of her cakes.
The parties would be fun, if a little too public,
though it was usually followed by a
disappointing gift. Following the dinner, at the
opening of the gifts, a silent thought of "never
get what I want" would be hidden behind the
expected birthday smile. This year however, he
got exactly what he had wanted and so the
memory of that was glued to the place where he
was, and Mary's diner had been one of his
favorite places ever since. He and his inseparable
friend Johnny would stop by for a soda after
school or a lunch of the oversized club
sandwiches in the middle of their weekend
adventures. The ever-cheerful Mary always
willing to look at the interesting rocks they'd
found in a stream or listen to the exciting tales
of how far they'd ridden their bikes into the
forest and the things they'd seen.

For Officer Vlad, his favorite memory of the
place was the first time he saw Tegan. Her family
had recently moved into town and the newly-
minted police officer had never seen her before.
He walked in, making his rounds and getting a
cup of coffee. Though he didn't really like coffee,
he thought all good cops should drink coffee. He
got up to the counter, where the take-out orders

were placed, next to the serving shelf where the prepared dishes basked under the heat lamps while waiting to be brought to the tables. Standing there next to the old-time cash register, waiting for Mary to furnish him with its familiar ding, he heard a small squeal. He turned to look, and he saw, to him, the most beautiful girl in the world. And this beautiful girl had a plate of spaghetti slopped over her head. There was a toddler across from her making a low, giggling sound. Officer Vlad thought that any girl who looked that pretty would have gotten angry, but to his surprise, she remained calm and only chided the small boy for his misbehavior. Impressed with her patience and calm, and thinking this would be a good way to introduce himself, he walked over and asked if he could be of any assistance. She thanked him and said that she was fine, and in his mind he thought decidedly so. He asked if her small dining friend was her son and when she explained that it was a baby-sitting favor she was doing for a neighbor he asked her out on the first date of many right there and then. They seemed to be made for each other and had been the town's "perfect couple" ever since.

For Mr. Dips the memory was just as strong, but not nearly so pleasant. This was where he sat for hours after the funeral for his wife. It was many years ago, but he remembered it as though it were yesterday. How he had found her slumped over the kitchen table, those silly coupons she loved to clip and save in her rose-embroidered coupon wallet, spread all around the table and floor. A freak cerebral hemorrhage was the doctor's explanation. A freak was what it left him. The favorite part of his life had been ripped away far too soon. With no desire to work or barely live anymore, he withdrew from most of life. He sat in the diner after the wake. Their closest friends filled with genuine despair at his situation. They sat away from him, giving him the space he wanted. He nursed their favorite meal to share there, Sheppard's Pie, until it was long cold and stale. Then he headed for the Empty Pump and never really left. He quit his job as a history professor, and instead strolled around town waiting for his end. The meager royalties from his rarely-used textbook "A History of Early Britain" allowed him to stay fed and buy a few drinks each evening.

On the whole though, the regulars of Mary's Diner had pleasant memories of the place. From weekly rituals with children and pancakes on Sunday morning, to young lovers and chocolate pie on Friday, to light lunches on Tuesdays with friends from the office, to Wednesday night dinners with surprisingly tolerable in-laws.

On a Thursday, just during the noon-day rush, Mr. Dips finished with his once-a-week meal out, and as he was going up to pay his bill, he noticed a spider web in the corner of the serving shelf. From his vantage point, it was perfectly back dropped by the dark shadow made by a large bowl of minestrone soup and brilliantly lit by the warming lamps above. A half-mumbled comment by him to Mary, who had just gotten to the register, brought forth a smile and a louder reply of "Spider web? You know, dear, that's to keep the flies out of the soup." A chuckle from some of the nearer patrons blended back into the sounds of clanking spoons and casual conversation.

A few of the guests' head tilted up as in thought and then glanced around. After a moment they were back attending to their meals. Mr. Dips, his brain not yet addled by the drinks he had each evening, looked around at these friendly and familiar people.

He noticed a few spots of distinctive red transmission fluid on the pant legs of Wilfred Barclay, the local artist in wood. His totem pole and soaring eagle creations brought forth from logs and stumps were a popular attraction at fairs and festivals all over the state. It was well-known in town that Willy didn't own a car, or even drive, his aging mother driving him when he needed it.

Mr. Dips also noticed loose hairs of fur on the back of Mr. Namari's light-blue coveralls. He was pretty sure the Namari family did not have any pets, nor were they likely to have any fur coats, as Mr. Namari was one of those rare plumbers who charged a reasonable fee. That and having to feed and clothe their six children made luxuries like a fur coat improbable.

A fledgling realization in Mr. Dips' mind was brought higher while passing Johnny's mother, who had just entered. He noticed the distinct smell of stale cigarettes on her brown pea-coat, and he knew for a fact that neither she, nor anyone else in her family, smoked.

Chief Jardem took that moment to walk through the door. Every one stopped talking and eating for the length of one heartbeat, then turned right back to what they were doing. The chief nodded to Mr. Dips, waved to a few people inside, and went to sit down.

Old Mr. Wardor was passing by on the sidewalk as Mr. Dips stepped out into the sun. The old barrister was taking a drink from a bottle of water. There was no bright logo on it. Mr. Dips looked from the aging lawyer with his dark-blue bowtie back into the diner.

His eyes passed from face to face. Most had smiles on them. Some were deeply engrossed in conversation; others were staring casually out one of the large windows. He'd known most of these people either all of their lives or all of his life. The idea that they would act in so daring a fashion to protect what they saw as their way of life was at first quite foreign. But as he thought more about it, he knew he was right. He knew what they had done. He had heard about the strange goings-on of late in the quiet, little town. He knew then and there that these people, all fine, regular folk had been a web. They had been a web to keep the annoying, bothersome flies out of the Boudton soup.

Mr. Dips walked down Main Street, with a little more bounce in his step than usual, and decided to see how the roses were getting along.

94380499R00076

Made in the USA
Columbia, SC
23 April 2018